# The Jaffa Cartel

J. TERRY JOHNSON

FOREWORD BY JOHN ASHTON

*The Jaffa Cartel*



Editing by Jen Boles

Cover and interior design by Word-2-Kindle

Published in the United States of America

ISBN: 9798839795761

1. Literature and Fiction: Crime
2. Literature and Fiction: Adventure

8.1.22

# Dedication

With great respect, I dedicate *The Jaffa Cartel* to Dino Roussos and Greg Neill, two fervent ambassadors for the gospel of Jesus Christ and men who may find themselves loosely profiled in the pages of this book. They are passionate laborers in the kingdom of God and have had a profound influence upon all who have come their way. I am in debt to both.

# Acknowledgments

Finding the inspirational spark to create any work of art is often a serendipitous occurrence. It may come from a word spoken by a friend or an encounter with a stranger on a faraway trip. When we least expect it, a light bulb illuminates the cobwebs in our minds, and *voila*! The wheels begin to turn.

When Cassie Peeples, the daughter-in-law of our friends and neighbors, Maurice and Gayla Peeples, gave my wife and me a copy of her first published book, *I'll Wash My Hair with Snow*, I knew the genre that I wanted to explore in my next writing adventure. A mystery novel. It looked like fun, and it was. Thank you, Cassie, for providing the stimulus I needed to write this book.

Jen Boles graciously consented to be my copyeditor. I engaged her services through Reedsy, an online marketplace, filled with talented professionals who can help with almost any facet of publishing a book. She sharpened the grammar in my original draft and brought greater clarity to the narrative.

It was my pleasure to work with the professional team at Word-2-Kindle that designed the cover, formatted the manuscript, and arranged for the finished copy to be uploaded for publication. They made the technical side of the publishing puzzle much easier for me to navigate.

Finally, I am truly honored that film star John Ashton wrote the foreword to *The Jaffa Cartel*. You remember him from his roles in *Beverly Hills Cop* (*I* and *II*), *Midnight Run*, and many other films. My favorite John Ashton movie is *Little Big League* in which he portrays a Major League Baseball coach for the Minnesota Twins. Humorous, entertaining, and pure fun for a baseball fan. John is one of the best character actors in Hollywood. And a big shout out to my brother-in-law, Brooks Mitchell, who leaned upon his friendship with John to make the request on my behalf. I owe you one, Bubba.

# Introduction

Would you believe a pre-school teacher was the person who introduced me to the diabolical act of murder? Yes, my Sunday School class was studying the Genesis account of Cain killing his brother Abel. The thought of someone taking another person's life was two or three steps higher on the intensity ladder than lessons we had learned about *sharing* and *obeying our parents*. Telling the age-old story, Wilma Clark had the class's undivided attention.

A few years later when my parents bought our family's first television set, I became hooked on Western movies. Stagecoach drivers shot their rifles at the Indians who returned fire using their bows and arrows. The Lone Ranger and Tonto were always bringing some murderous outlaw to justice. So were Roy Rogers and Hopalong Cassidy. Murdering someone lost its novelty, but never its wickedness or its mystery.

As I grew older, my preference for cowboy stories was replaced by another genre of screenwriting. Perry Mason and Della Street, who could solve murder mysteries in sixty minutes or less, became my favorite television attraction. Mason's client was always charged with murder by Lt. Arthur Tragg and Los Angeles District

Attorney Hamilton Burger, but before the hour was over, the real murderer was exposed by the masterful defense attorney.

What made *Perry Mason* one of the most acclaimed programs of its time? It was not the acting, to be sure, although Raymond Burr was certainly credible in his title role. Nor was it the stage sets or the black and white cinematography. No, it was the mystery and intrigue surrounding the criminal activity. Everyone loves a good murder mystery.

Erle Stanley Gardener wrote the collection of crime stories that inspired the *Perry Mason* series. He had a gift for developing a compelling plot with twists and turns that kept the reader spellbound until the very last chapter. Agatha Christie and Arthur Conan Doyle became literary legends using this genre and since their time, murder mysteries have become a staple among modern writers of fiction.

Since retiring from a career in university administration, I have found pleasure in creative writing. Much of what I have written has been for my own amusement. An illustrated children's book, a cookbook, a daily devotional guide, a chronicle of church history, a collection of poems, and a novella about baseball are a few of the works I have published over the past twenty years. Each had its own challenges and rewards. But until I sat down to write *The Jaffa Cartel*, developing a storyline had never been so much fun. At the end of each chapter, even I was anxious to see what events might transpire in the next one.

Sit back and enjoy the ride. *The Jaffa Cartel* will take you on a journey from the hills of South-Central Texas to the skyscrapers of New York City, and from the antiquities of Athens, Greece, to the Israeli port city of Old Jaffa. Somewhere along the way, a murder takes place.

# Contents

# Foreword

I love to read a good story. Who doesn't? But when that story blends captivating scenes from international locations with the criminal behavior of a ruthless cartel, I'm hooked. Even the title of this book, *The Jaffa Cartel*, piqued my interest from page one.

Over the years, I have read my share of fiction, whether written as books or screenplays. Most have provided me a moment to escape from the real world and allowed me to identify with characters and circumstances far removed from those I encounter in my daily life. *The Jaffa Cartel* is the perfect case in point. From the slums of Warsaw, Poland, to the ancient port city of Jaffa, Israel, and to the beautiful city of antiquities, Athens, Greece, I sank deeper and deeper into the plot of this stylish murder mystery.

What surprised me about the book was the way its author, J. Terry Johnson, was able to weave transcendental thought into the narrative, adding a dimension of ideas not normally found in this genre. The characters are real. Their struggles with the unexpected occurrences in life resonate with readers who have had similar experiences. In the darkest of times, silver linings offer hope.

If this book were ever adapted into a movie script, I could see myself playing the role of Inspector Giorgos Papadakis. Persistent. Methodical. Instinctive. He is a man on a mission and up for any challenge. I relish playing a character that knits the storyline together, without necessarily having to be the lead actor. The inspector is my kind of man.

Taking a few hours to read *The Jaffa Cartel* is well worth your time. I heartily recommend it.

*John Ashton*

# 1

# The Field Trip

### Jaffa

On a Wednesday afternoon in April, Leah Melamed and her classmates from the Golda Meir Elementary School in Jaffa, Israel, were on a field trip to the Museum of Antiquities. The small stone building was located near the city's old port on the waterfront. Ms. Elena Rubenstein's third-grade class made an annual pilgrimage to the Old City, learning its history and absorbing the culture of their hometown. The tour was one of the highlights of the school year.

Jaffa was a city that had belonged to marauding armies from all over the globe. The Egyptians, the Greeks, the Romans, the Crusaders and Saladin, and even Napoleon Bonaparte besieged the city at one time. If an empire builder had not sacked Jaffa, he was something less than a world-class conqueror. The city was a doormat for ambitious sovereigns.

The museum's knowledgeable docent, Ruth Friedman, was a retired teacher who enjoyed entertaining young children with the stories of Jaffa's past.

"You live in a city that has existed for almost four thousand years," Ms. Friedman began her familiar spiel. "It hasn't always been known as Tel Aviv-Yafo as we call it today. Centuries ago, our city was named *Joppa* and more recently, *Jaffa*. Our smaller city merged with Tel Aviv in 1950 and the two communities were blended into one, much larger metropolis."

Ms. Friedman continued her colorful account of Jaffa's history for another fifteen minutes before releasing the class to explore the museum and its creative exhibits. Leah and her friends loved the whimsical dolls on display in antique glass cabinets. The boys spent extra time in the mariner section of the museum where artifacts from ancient ships had been collected over hundreds of years. They imagined themselves as warriors on one of those ships, sailing into Jaffa's famous port, prepared for heroic adventures in a new land.

After leaving the museum, the children lined up in front of the scenic harbor where Ms. Rubenstein took a class photograph. She would have prints made at a local pharmacy and present each child with a copy on the last day of school. It was her farewell gift to the class and a good reminder of a special day spent in Old Jaffa.

Leah enjoyed school. She was an above-average student who excelled in history and mathematics. If she had a major deficiency, it would be her lack of social skills. She had grown up as the only child in a dysfunctional family.

Ramon Melamed, Leah's father, worked as a day laborer in the local citrus fields but had a tough time holding a steady job because of his alcohol dependence. Her mother had problems of her own. Addicted to cocaine, Mary Melamed had been in rehabilitation programs for most of her adult life. In place of her unstable home life, Golda Meir Elementary School had become Leah's "happy place."

As Leah walked home from school that day, she was anxious to tell her mother what she had seen at the museum. Her favorite recollection was of the man dressed as a pirate, like the ones who pillaged the coast of Jaffa during the late 1800s. The bearded sailor had the obligatory black eyepatch covering one eye and a live parrot sitting on his shoulder. With some coaxing from the students, the pirate was able to get the parrot to *talk*. Leah loved the theatrics of it all.

The Melamed home was one in a series of rowhouses that lined both sides of a narrow residential street. Leah could hear her mother's screams from the moment she turned the corner, a block away from her house. It was not the first time she had been welcomed home to a family crisis. She began to run as she approached her front doorsteps and burst into the living room to find her mother throwing dishes at the kitchen wall. The scene was all too familiar.

Mary was ranting and cursing as she always did when spiraling out of control.

"He's done it again! Gone, Leah. Gone! If I could, I'd kill him."

Leah had heard the threats before. Whenever her father had gone on a bender, Mary threw one of these fits and doubled down on her use of cocaine. This was not going to be a comfortable evening in the Melamed house. Leah began to cry.

"What are you crying for," Mary shrieked at the young girl, now clutching her mother's waist? "Get away from me!"

"Momma, he'll come back."

"I don't want him back! I hope he never comes back!" And with that she shoved Leah away from her side, pushing her into a large wooden buffet.

Leah's head hit hard against an opened drawer on the piece of olive wood furniture. Blood began running down her cheek, blending with the tears that flowed more freely from her eyes. She stumbled to her feet and ran out the front door. The pain was unbearable–both the physical pain and the emotional trauma.

Three doors down the street, a neighbor was sweeping her front sidewalk. She had also heard Mary's ranting and her fits of rage. Now, seeing a young girl bolting out of the Melamed's house and running toward her, the woman dropped her broom and grabbed Leah by the arm. Blood smeared on the woman's hand as she tried to brush Leah's hair back and tend to the wound.

"Come inside, dear. We need to get you to a doctor."

# # # # # #

Two months had passed since Leah's unforgettable night in the hospital. Doctors treated her in the emergency room, stitching up the gash on the side of her head. She was held for observation overnight and released to a local juvenile care center the next afternoon. Mary had been arrested and charged with assault and endangering a child. The court had placed her in a drug rehabilitation center to await trial for the criminal charges. Ramon had skipped town and was never heard from again.

The summer heat was oppressive in Jaffa on the day court convened to determine whether Leah would remain at the juvenile center or be released into the custody of a foster family. Neither of her natural parents was present at the hearing. Four witnesses were called to testify about Leah's condition, past and present. The first was Regina Warwitz, the neighbor who had rescued Leah and had taken her to the hospital.

"It's not the first time I have heard screams and yelling coming from the Melamed residence," Warwitz said. "I have worried for months what would become of this child. Last April, when I saw her running down the street, bleeding from whatever happened between her and her mother, I knew I had to do something to help her. That's when I called the police and took Leah to the hospital."

The court also heard from a Jaffa police officer who responded to Warwitz's call for help. He described the scene inside the Melamed house, having found broken dishes on the floor and Leah's blood on the buffet's drawer. Next, a hospital official testified to Leah's condition when she was admitted to the emergency room. The wound was described as severe, having fractured a bone near Leah's eye. Twelve stitches had been used to sew up the gash.

Leah's caseworker at the juvenile center recounted the observations of her client's behavior in the center and the results of testing that had been administered.

"She is a bright young lady, withdrawn socially, but able to function in society if she has support. Her father cannot be found, and her mother's addiction is a major concern. It would not be best to remand her into the custody of her mother under any circumstances."

After having heard from the witnesses, Judge Rudy Weiss thanked them for their testimonies and for their interest in Leah Melamed's well-being.

"There is one more witness I would like to hear from this afternoon. Ms. Miriam Steinmann, would you like to share something with us today," Judge Weiss asked?

Miriam Steinmann was Leah Melamed's fifty-five-year-old maternal grandmother. She lived in Jaffa, working at a dry goods store while raising Leah's aunt and Mary Melamed's younger sister, Rachel Steinmann. She and Rachel had been partially estranged from Mary and Ramon for more than five years. Miriam rose from her seat on the back row of the courtroom and slowly made her way toward the bench.

Judge Weiss smiled at the unassuming woman as she stood before him. "Ms. Steinmann, I understand that you have something you would like to share with us today. Please, have a seat."

Miriam paused for a moment before responding to the judge. "Thank you, your honor. I'm sorry this meeting has been necessary this afternoon. Leah is a sweet child and life has not been easy for her in the past few years. She deserves better. Due to circumstances with her parents, I have not been able to help as much as I would have liked. I love Leah and believe that I could provide her with a safe home. I live with my daughter Rachel. She is seventeen and has told me that she will help me raise Leah if the court allows me to have custody of her until she is grown and on her own. I have come today to make that request."

# 2

# The Green Wasps

**Poland**

Life was not easy in the ghettos of Warsaw, Poland. Crime in the streets was not criminal. It was *survival*. Gangs of teenage boys roamed the city at will, daring the police to make an issue of their menacing behavior.

Aleksy Jablonski had grown up in these neighborhoods. At the age of fifteen, he had dropped out of school and had run away from his poverty-stricken family, choosing to fend for himself in a crapshoot on the streets. Within a year, he had become a leader of The Green Wasps, a roguish gang that terrorized passersby on the sidewalks by day and ransacked business establishments that were closed at night. His size alone, six feet three inches and two hundred sixty pounds, was threatening to all who stood in his way.

In addition to their daily regimen of committing thefts and assaults, the gangs were also involved in the marketing of illegal drugs. Drug trafficking had become more prevalent in Warsaw since Poland had distanced itself from the shadow of the former Soviet Union. Greater freedom brought with it opportunistic entrepreneurs who transformed the nation from being a semi-police state into a haven for drug peddlers and mob bosses who excelled in evading local authorities.

Aleksy was up to his armpits in the illegal drug trade. He had begun as most do: first as a user, then as a dealer, and finally as an overseer of a territory for which he had exclusive sales rights. Using his powers of persuasion, he had assembled a formidable team of runners who pushed the drugs and attracted new recruits for their cause.

In the same year when Leah Melamed made her third-grade field trip to the Museum of Antiquities in Old Jaffa, Aleksy and the Green Wasps met their match on the streets of Warsaw. A rival gang had begun to encroach upon the Wasps' neighborhoods, brazenly peddling their own supplies of heroin and cocaine as if no one cared about their intrusion. Aleksy called a meeting of the Wasp leaders.

"Game on," Aleksy rallied his comrades. "It's going down tonight behind the Gorski Warehouse. Be there with your teams, armed and ready for a tough night."

A bloody battle between the two factions ensued in the warehouse district, leaving dozens of teenage boys suffering knife wounds and other bodily injuries. Aleksy, himself, was severely slashed by a razor-sharp blade that caught him behind his right shoulder. The Wasps had been soundly defeated, never to dominate the streets again. It closed a chapter in Aleksy's life and set the stage for a new one.

Without a gang to lead and needing income to survive, Aleksy walked and hitched rides on a 420-kilometer trek north, using the highways and byroads that led to the Baltic Sea. The teenager was tough and resourceful. He ate what he could find, stealing fruit and vegetables from gardens and scavenging trash bins in alleyways. One week after leaving Warsaw, he arrived in Poland's leading port city, Gdansk.

International shipping was the heartbeat of commerce in Gdansk. It did not take Aleksy long to find the employment offices of major industries that operated from the busy port. Working on a tip he had received from a man he had met in a public park, Aleksy made a call on the offices of Maritime Shipping.

"Is this the place where I can get a job?" he inquired, poking his head into a messy office, cluttered with wastepaper and reeking of cigarette smoke. Aleksy had never held a real job or worked anywhere other than his brief career as a *capo* with the Wasps.

A rosy-cheeked Pole raised his head from the paperwork on his desk. "You can fill out an application like everyone else. We don't hand out jobs like they were shopping fliers on the street corner." The man rose from his desk and walked to a filing cabinet where he took out a folder. "Here, take this form and fill it out. You can use that table in the corner."

Aleksy sat at the table and studied the form. He was perplexed by the process. *What should I put down as my address? Do I tell them that I did not graduate from high school? Who should I list as my previous employer?* So far, all he had written on the form was his name.

"Is there something wrong," the man asked?

"Not really. You see, I just arrived in town and haven't found a place to stay," Aleksy began to explain. "I haven't had a real job before."

"Where are you from?"

"Warsaw."

"And what kind of job are you looking for?"

"Anything you need for me to do."

The man took special notice of Aleksy's size, imagining what it would be like having the young man's strong back employed on Maritime's loading docks. "Let me help you with that form," he said. "I think I know a job that will be just right for you."

Jakub Wosniak was in his early twenties and had been working at Maritime Shipping for five years. As an experienced dock worker, Jakub was given the task of mentoring Aleksy, teaching him the basic skills of loading and unloading cargo from piers to ships and vice versa.

The two men were compatible as co-workers and became friends. Jakub even invited Aleksy to share his third-floor apartment until he could find a place of his own.

Aleksy was surprised at how much he enjoyed having a full-time job. It established structure to his days and added dignity to his sense of personal worth. He proved to be an excellent stevedore, capable of doing half again as much work as most of the men on the docks. The company rewarded him with praise and an occasional bonus. That part of his new life was good.

What Aleksy did not like was *Gdansk*. The city was dreary, and the winters were brutal. Other than Jakub, he had few friends and no life apart from his work with Maritime. He began to get an itch to move on to new adventures in a warmer climate. One evening after a long day on the docks, Jakub brought home a lifeline.

"Did you hear the news about the company's new operation in Greece?" Jakub said.

"No, what's the deal?"

"Maritime is opening a branch office in Piraeus, Greece, and will be taking applications for some of our employees to help get the new venture started. You interested?"

"You bet, I am," Aleksy answered immediately. "Anything to get me out of here. Where do we apply?"

"Well, I don't think I'll be moving to Greece with you, but if you're interested, check with the personnel office in the morning. They're taking the applications."

Two months later, Aleksy Jablonski was on a freighter, bound for Greece. He never looked back on his decision to leave Poland.

# 3

# Jaffa Industries

### Jaffa – Years Later

Nine years had passed since Judge Weiss granted custody of Leah Melamed to her maternal grandmother. What Miriam Steinmann lacked in material resources, she more than compensated for with loving care and encouragement for her granddaughter. Leah's teenage years could be described as *pedestrian*, at best: stable, but nothing fancy. She did not date or show much interest in boys. Her classmates described her as a *loner*.

The only extra-curricular activity Leah enjoyed was participating in the high school gymnastics program. The physical training routine kept her toned and strong. She had performed academically well enough in high school to graduate but showed no interest in pursuing a college degree. Full-time employment was in her near-term future.

Leah's best friend was her Aunt Rachel. Although separated by eight years, the girls shared a bedroom and spent a reasonable amount of time together when Leah first arrived at her grandmother's house. Rachel had been especially supportive of Leah, treating her like a kid sister. When they were not doing homework or tending to chores, they made trips to the park or visited the local drugstore where many of Rachel's friends liked to mingle. If certain boys were there, however, Rachel would buy Leah a soda and a comic book, expecting her to stay out of sight.

Rachel graduated from high school two years after her niece had moved in. Six months later, she married her high school boyfriend, Andrew Braun, and left her mother's house. Andrew was committed to pursuing a military career and was away on deployments for six to eight months of the year. When Andrew was away for an extended period, Rachel often stayed over with her mother and Leah.

Leah's mother and father were no longer a part of her life. Ramon Melamed had not been seen since the day he left, nine years ago. Mary Melamed had spent eight agonizing years in an Israeli prison. Although she was released a year before Leah's senior year in high school, Mary had chosen to keep her distance. Leah felt no animosity toward her mother, but neither was she drawn to her. Separation was the best arrangement for all members of the family.

One morning while Leah was at her senior accounting class, she received a memorandum from a clerk in the school's administrative offices asking her to visit with the occupational guidance counselor at her earliest convenience. Before taking her lunch break, Leah dropped by the office of Herman Kratz and knocked on his door.

"Come in," a booming voice rang from the other side of the closed door.

"Mr. Kratz, I am Leah Melamed. You wanted to see me?"

"I do, Ms. Melamed. Please, have a seat." Kratz was a large man, bald, and wearing dark-rimmed glasses. He was old enough to be Leah's grandfather.

"I understand you may be looking for a job after you graduate. Is that correct?"

"Yes, sir. I have been working part-time at Goldman's Grocery but will need to have a full-time job after I graduate."

"Good. I have recently learned about a position that will be available this summer with one of our finest local employers. Have you ever heard of Jaffa Industries?"

"No, sir."

"Well, trust me. They are a fine company that has a reputation for paying good wages to their employees and providing them with excellent benefits. They are looking for a high school graduate who has good marks in mathematics and business. Your teachers speak highly of you, and I have noticed your grades in math and accounting have been superb. I think it might be a fit. Would you be interested in visiting with one of their representatives next week?"

"Yes, I would. Thank you, Mr. Kratz."

"Alright, I will send you a memo with the date, time, and place for the interview. It will be here in my office or our conference room. Here is a flyer describing the interview process, what to wear, and other suggestions. Also, I have a brochure from Jaffa Industries. Read it thoroughly, Ms. Melamed, before the interview. I think you will find it helpful. Any questions?"

"No. But thank you again, Mr. Kratz. I look forward to learning more about the job."

# # # # # #

Three years had passed since Leah was hired by Jaffa Industries. Her official title was, "shipping clerk." The role called for her to take purchase orders and invoices, turn them into freight documents, and see that the products being sent were physically accounted for in the shipment. Jaffa Industries sold its electronic equipment to buyers throughout the world. She had bad dreams about products purchased by customers in France ending up in Argentina, but so far, nothing like that had ever happened.

Leah could not have been more pleased with her starting salary at Jaffa. It was five times what she had made working part-time at the grocery mart. Furthermore, the company had given her a wage increase every six months since she had been on the payroll. Her take-home pay was enough for Leah and her grandmother to live comfortably, so she prevailed upon "Bubbe" to retire from her job at the downtown store. From now on, her grandmother could cook, clean the house, and tend to her flower gardens in the backyard.

One Monday morning in October, Ishmael Reuben, the Executive Vice President of Jaffa Industries appeared in the shipping office. He gathered the employees into a conference room where he broke the news of a shake-up in the department.

"Leonard Ambersohn has been terminated as manager of our shipping operations. The department will now report to Yosef Cohen, our new manager. We are implementing some new systems today. Mr. Ambersohn chose not to accommodate those changes. I'll just leave it at that."

"Furthermore," Reuben continued, "Jaffa Industries has a new transport agreement with Maritime Shipping and will be working closely with their operations in Europe. Under our new contract, much of the product that we sell abroad will be shipped from our warehouses in Jaffa to the port in Piraeus, Greece. From there, it will be routed to its final destination. Mr. Cohen is well briefed on the details and can answer any questions you may have."

The new contract was of little importance to Leah. She still needed to prepare the paperwork, match orders with products being shipped, and have the ultimate destination point reflected on the freight bills. The only difference was that the initial shipping address was almost always *Piraeus, Greece.*

Leah was surprised, however, to learn that Yosef Cohen was going to be her new boss. Cohen had been an aide in Ishmael Reuben's office for many years. She thought of him being one of the "suits" rather than a department manager. *Time would tell whether he was equipped to handle this new role,* she thought, trying to digest his unexpected promotion.

# 4

# The Promotion

### Jaffa – Three Years Later

At first, Leah was unfazed by the changes made in Jaffa Industries' Shipping Department. Yosef Cohen was a capable manager, treated the employees with respect, and allowed each to do the job that had been assigned. She liked his style, and because he was much younger than her former boss, she related well to his directives. What sealed the deal for her, however, was the three percent merit pay raise he gave her after her initial performance review. It motivated her to work longer hours to prove herself worthy of the confidence he had displayed.

The work itself was the same as always: invoice matching products, freight documents prepared properly, with the only new wrinkle being the routing of all shipments through the port in Piraeus, Greece. Maritime Shipping had sent Jaffa new containers that were quite different from the ones they had used in the past. If they did the job, the containers were not a problem for Leah. For her, one kind of bin was as good as another.

Leah was surprised, however, when Yosef stopped at her desk one afternoon and asked if he could take her to dinner that night. She was unaccustomed to having any man show special interest in her personally. His initiative was not something that had appeared on her radar screen.

"Would seven o'clock work for you?" Yosef asked.

"I can be ready then." And the date was on.

Dinner one night led to a second dinner date the week after. In the third week, they spent an evening in Tel Aviv at a musical theater. The buzz of it all was exciting for Leah. She found Yosef attractive, a gentleman, and generous in his compliments of her and her work at Jaffa. Although he had not made any romantic advances, she was satisfied to keep the relationship on a friendship basis. That seemed to work best for him as well.

One Friday afternoon before operations at Jaffa Industries shut down for Shabbat, Yosef approached Leah while she was inspecting cartons that were ready to be placed in the Maritime containers for transport to Greece.

"Can I pick you up Saturday night around six or so?" Yosef asked.

"Sure. Where are we going?"

"It's a surprise, but a good surprise. I have a proposal to make. I think you'll like it."

"I'll be ready."

Leah had rehearsed the conversation multiple times in her mind. *A surprise. A proposal to make. You'll like it.*

The suspense had made her uneasy as she waited for Yosef to drive up to her doorstep. As was his custom, he was right on time.

"Let's get a bite of dinner and then I have something to show you at the office," Yosef said as Leah slipped into her seatbelt.

"The office? Really?"

"Yes, the office," Yosef said with a smirk and a wink.

Shrimp scampi at The Happy Clam was delicious, but Leah did not have much appetite. The *surprise* kept bouncing around in her head and was beginning to upset her stomach. During the meal, she and Yosef teased each other as couples do in the initial stages of dating. The art of conversation with a man was becoming easier for Leah. She liked Yosef or at least the attention he had been giving to her. As they were leaving the restaurant, he reached for her hand.

The offices at Jaffa Industries were closed until eight o'clock the next morning. The buildings were dark with only a few lights shining in the parking lots. Yosef pulled his Ferrari into one of the many open spaces, turned off the motor, and helped Leah open her door. They walked to the shipping department's side entrance where Yosef fumbled with his keys until he found the one that fit. The couple stepped inside.

Other than the building's emergency exit signage, the only light that was on in the warehouse came from

Yosef's office. It was located on an elevated landing that was five feet higher than the freight room floor. Yosef led the way up the stairs with Leah a half-step behind. To her surprise, Ishmael Reuben was seated in Yosef's chair, waiting for the couple to arrive.

"I told you I had a surprise," Yosef beamed.

"Good evening, Leah," Reuben smiled, looking straight into the young woman's eyes. "You look lovely tonight. Please, you and Yosef have a seat."

"Thank you." Leah could not think of anything more to say to a person of Reuben's status in the company.

"I have been getting excellent reports from Yosef about your work in the department. You deserve to be rewarded for those efforts and that is why I am here tonight."

Leah was embarrassed. She had wanted to make a good impression on Yosef but had never thought of his making comments on her work to officers in the company. *What could this mean?*

"Let me get straight to the point," Reuben continued. "Leah, Yosef and I want to make you our assistant shipping manager at Jaffa Industries. You are already more productive than anyone else in the department. You deserve the promotion."

"Really? Me? Assistant manager?"

"That's right. And here is the best part, Leah. Effective immediately, your salary is being doubled."

“Oh, no! I don’t know what to say. Thank you, Mr. Reuben, thank you. How can I ever repay you?”

“Well, there are a few additional responsibilities and some new procedures to implement, but I’m sure you will handle them easily enough. Yosef will explain all of that to you.” Reuben paused for a moment.

“By the way, I need to clarify something about the pay increase. You will continue to receive your normal paycheck from the company at the end of the month, but Yosef will also give you an envelope with cash that will match the amount of the company’s check.” Reuben stood to leave.

“It’s been my pleasure, Leah. Best to you in your new position.”

Leah and Yosef bid Reuben goodbye and sat back down in their chairs.

“You knew this was coming?” she inquired.

“Yes, but Mr. Reuben wanted to break the good news to you personally. He takes a special interest in several employees that occupy key roles in the company. He has chosen you to be among that group. Now, let me explain some of the new responsibilities and procedures he mentioned a moment ago. This is important.”

Yosef pulled a new set of shipping documents from a file drawer and laid them out on top of his desk. He explained that from now on, Leah was to use the pricing guide found on the new forms rather than the prices found in the company's catalog. *That shouldn't be a problem*, she thought as Yosef continued with the tutorial.

After spending time with the new paperwork, Yosef took Leah to the warehouse floor where Maritime Shipping's new containers were stacked on pallets. He showed her the secret compartments she had never seen before. In fact, she never would have noticed them had Yosef not demonstrated how they could be opened. The night had become more intriguing than she ever could have imagined.

# 5

# Heavenly Sunlight

**Pecan Village – Sunday, June 5**

Heavenly sunbeams streamed through the stained-glass windows of the Pecan Village Community Church where more than two hundred members had assembled for Sunday morning worship. They imagined themselves a "city set on a hill," spreading sunshine and good tidings to all they met. It was a sweet fellowship of believers who lived out their faith among their fellow residents in the rustic Texas Hill Country.

A quick glance of the church property suggested that the congregation catered to affluent families. It was located adjacent to Travis Park, the town's most desirable venue for outside social gatherings. Large SUVs, foreign import sedans, and a few high-dollar pick-up trucks filled the freshly striped parking lot. Texas Longhorn decals and bumper stickers outnumbered other university logos, two-to-one.

The church building, although modest in size, was constructed five years ago in this sleepy Central Texas town and the members had spared little expense in providing for its design and furnishings. A large porte-cochere covered the driveway at the entry doors, protecting the parishioners whenever they arrived in inclement weather. State-of-the-art audio-visual equipment could be found in the sanctuary and every classroom. A fully equipped kitchen allowed for meals to be served in the spacious fellowship hall and the ministerial offices would rival the executive suites of most business enterprises in Pecan Village.

A comfortable building, however, does not guarantee that all is well with a church community. Although it was meant to provide an uplifting experience, each Sunday morning service, lacking any hint of spontaneity, had become a replica of the weeks before. The order of worship followed a tired and predictable template. Barry Garman, the local high school's band director, always led the congregational singing. All heads were bowed for public prayers, the audience stood whenever the Scriptures were read, and participation in the communion service had become nothing more than a weekly ritual. In keeping with the admonishment of the Apostle Paul, everything at PVC was done "decently and in order," but rarely with any variation.

Lance Arnold, the local preacher, was highly respected by the congregation, but he was not professionally trained in ministry. He had graduated thirty years ago from Baylor University's School of Law. While in law school, he had interned with Williams, Sanger, and Fields, a prominent law firm in Houston, and had accepted the partners' offer for a permanent position upon his graduation from Baylor. Most of his annual income was still derived from investments he had acquired while practicing law, but a legal career had never been his life's ambition.

An itch to preach had been planted in a tender heart by his paternal grandmother when Lance was in elementary school. Over the years, he had been drawn into church work and especially relished the opportunity to teach Sunday morning Bible classes. On a few occasions when the regular preacher was away, Lance had even been asked to preach and found the experience to his liking.

Now, full-time in ministry, Lance replayed his grandmother's words often as he prepared his weekly lessons and labored tirelessly among his parishioners.

"You're my preacher boy," she would whisper sweetly in his ear. "Study to show yourself approved unto God," he could hear her quoting one of her favorite passages from the *Bible*.

*The congregation is in good voice this morning*, Lance mused, as Barry led an up-tempo hymn featuring a strong alto lead. Mildred Simmons never let such an opportunity pass. She belted out the lyrics as if she were calling cattle to the barn for feeding. Newcomers always glanced her way when Mildred was in her moment.

At the close of the hymn, Barry announced an invitation song, and Lance, *Bible* in hand, stepped up to the pulpit. He took a second to peruse the audience, acknowledging visitors with a nod of his head and making a mental note of any conspicuous absences among the membership. These were *his* people. He thought of them as *family*.

Sam and Belinda Sanders, with six children and Belinda's parents visiting from nearby Austin, filled the second row. Sam was the owner of Super Buns, Pecan Village's finest bakery. Lance made it a point to drop in on Sam at least once a week to rehash the local sports scene and to make sure the apple fritters were as good as he had remembered them being the week before. The twosome also had a standing tee time on Mondays for a weekly round of golf at Lone Spur, the local municipal course. Both men were addicted to the game and carried single-digit handicaps.

Toward the back of the auditorium sat Leonard England, a crotchety old man who delighted in finding fault with Lance and his sermons. Leonard had not had a fresh thought in the past thirty years. His perspective on religion was seen totally through the rearview mirror. If a doctrinal position was not identical to what Leonard had been taught by his grandfather, it was *unscriptural*, if not outright *heresy*. And do not get him started on the use of any translation of the *Bible* other than the King James

Version. He was known for having equated some of the more recent versions to punk rock and video porn.

To his credit, however, there was a genuine soft spot in Leonard's heart. He meant no harm to anyone. The members knew that Leonard would be present every time the church doors opened. Weddings. Funerals. Prayer meetings. He attended them all. And pot-luck luncheons? Leonard loved any meal served in the new fellowship hall.

Seated in their regular pew, center aisle, and middle of the auditorium were William G. Blevins and his wife Donna. Their children were grown and living in the Dallas-Ft. Worth metroplex. Bill and Lance had been classmates at Baylor Law. Both had graduated with honors but thereafter, had gone their separate ways–Lance to Houston and Bill to Dallas.

Ten years ago, Bill left his law firm in Dallas and moved to Pecan Village where he set up a private practice. Upon learning that Lance was preaching for a small church that was meeting temporarily in a public-school auditorium, Bill and Donna joined the fellowship and became the church's most generous benefactors. The new building would not have been possible had it not been for a substantial gift from the Blevins family.

On this Sunday morning, Lance worked his way through an exegesis of the second chapter of Ephesians, noting with emphasis that *salvation was God's gift rather than something anyone earned.* It was a theme he preached often. His grandmother would have been proud because *grace* had been her calling card. At the close of Lance's sermon, Barry led the congregation in a hymn, after which Herbert Lampkin, one of the elders, offered a prayer, and the service was concluded.

As members and guests made their way into the spacious church foyer, Lance stood alone, smiling, and greeting all with a firm handshake. The ritual was a habit he had learned from older preachers who had been successful in keeping close tabs on their flocks. It was part of his shepherding regimen and a way for him to stay in touch with the joys and sorrows of the good folk who had been entrusted into his care.

"Good morning, Mildred," Lance chuckled as he gave the matronly woman a gentle hug. "Barry had us singing with the angels this morning."

"Your words are always so inspiring, Brother Arnold," Mildred responded. "A church can't get fed too much *grace*. Thank you for sharing from your heart this morning." Lance enjoyed the compliment, even though he knew Mildred would have had something nice to say even if he had preached a lesson on "The Perils of Hell."

Waiting patiently for Mildred to move on was Bill Blevins. He smiled and shook Lance's extended hand. "Another good lesson this morning," Bill said sincerely. "My bucket is full."

"Thanks, Bill. Always good to see you and Donna holding down that center aisle. What are the chances of your joining Sam and me for a round of golf tomorrow morning?"

"Regretfully, I'll have to pass," Bill sighed. "I have a business trip to Athens later this week and need to fly into New York tomorrow for a briefing with my client."

"A business trip to Greece?" Lance beamed. "You probably need to take the preacher along to carry your bags." They both laughed.

"Seriously, what kind of business do you have going on in Athens?" Lance probed.

Bill's face tightened in an expression of bewilderment. "Honestly, I don't know exactly what I'm in for. A client of mine has business operations in Europe and the Middle East. He has asked me to go with him and sit in on some meetings with trade partners. That's about all I know," he shrugged.

"Hope it goes well," Lance replied. "Let's get together when you come home, and you can tell me all about it. Safe travel!"

# 6

# Gnawing Questions

### New York City – Monday, June 6

The Burrows Tower was one of Manhattan's newer office buildings, dwarfed by a sea of incredibly tall skyscrapers and scarcely noticed except by those who happened to do business in its lavish suites and conference rooms. Triton International, a conglomerate with offices in Europe and the Middle East, had its headquarters in the Burrows, occupying floors fifteen through twenty-four. Among Triton's many clients was Lone Star Electronics (LSE), a privately owned sales company located in Dallas. William G. Blevins was the outside general counsel hired by LSE to assist the company with its international trade agreements.

Bill had arrived Monday afternoon at LaGuardia Airport and had taken a taxi to his favorite Manhattan hotel, the Marriott at Times Square. As much as he hated traveling to New York City, there was something exhilarating about being at the epicenter of the city's theater district. If Donna had been with him, he would have bought tickets for them to see one of the latest Broadway musicals. Being alone, however, he had chosen to spend the evening in his hotel room, reviewing a few files he had prepared for Tuesday's meeting with his client.

The Marriott's telephone alarm rang promptly at 6:30 a.m., Tuesday morning, rousing Bill from a restless sleep. After standing under a warm shower for ten revitalizing minutes, he toweled himself dry, partially dressed for the day, and called Donna. He let her know his schedule for the morning, inquired about hers, and promised to call her again when he got to Athens.

Allowing at least two hours of free time before his morning appointment, Bill retrieved copies of the *Wall Street Journal* and the *New York Times*, both of which had been placed outside his door by a bell clerk. He read the lead stories to begin his long day. It was a daily habit he had practiced since his years in law school.

The markets were mixed at the close of trade on Monday–the Dow down, the Nasdaq up, and the S&P up a point. The Greek economy was tanking, China was still making aggressive noises toward its neighbors in Southeast Asia, and the President was hosting seven state governors at the White House. The news of the day was hardly *new*. Bill finished dressing, packed his bags, and called for the bellman to retrieve his luggage and store it until he was ready to leave for the airport.

A Starbucks was located on Seventh Avenue, adjacent to the hotel. Bill decided to drop in for a bagel and a cup of Americano, calling that breakfast. He was looking forward to having some fresh baklava when he arrived in Greece. It was his all-time favorite pastry. If given the chance, he would bring home an authentic Greek baklava recipe for Sam to try out at Super Buns.

Checking his watch, Bill walked five blocks north to the Burrows, arriving at Triton's offices at 9:45 a.m., well in advance of his 10:00 a.m. meeting. He made it his practice to be prompt for every business engagement.

"William Blevins," he introduced himself to the receptionist who sat behind a semi-circular counter on the twenty-fourth floor. "I have a 10:00 o'clock appointment with Mr. Clyde Wilbanks and Mr. Herman Moore."

"Yes, Mr. Blevins," she said with a welcoming smile. "Mr. Wilbanks is expecting you. May I get you a cup of coffee?"

"Thanks, but no," he replied. "I just had my caffeine quota a few minutes ago at Starbucks."

The young lady, an attractive brunette in her late twenties, stood and motioned to an alcove adjacent to the lobby. "Please have a seat. Mr. Wilbanks will be with you shortly."

Bill sat on the cushioned armchair, thumbing mindlessly through the latest *New Yorker* magazine that he found on a square coffee table in front of him. The nature of the morning's meeting was still slightly unclear to him. He knew that Lone Star had been purchasing electronic parts through Triton and that Herman Moore was trying to eliminate a few steps in the supply chain. From what he had learned in prior conversations with the executive team at Lone Star, materials made by Jaffa Industries in Israel were being shipped to Greece and then to New York before arriving in Texas. One objective was to see if the delivery could be streamlined with parts being shipped directly from Tel Aviv to Dallas-Ft. Worth.

What was more troubling to Bill were the invoices and financial statements he had reviewed while doing his preparation for the overseas trip. Unless he was missing something, Lone Star was being charged more money for the Israeli parts than was printed in the Jaffa Industries' catalog and the shipping fees appeared to be exorbitant. He was sure a reasonable explanation would be forthcoming in this morning's meeting, or at the session scheduled for Thursday in Athens.

"Mr. Blevins?" A middle-aged woman, dressed in a stylish, burgundy suit emerged from a hallway and broke Bill's musing. He rose from his chair and nodded. "Mr. Wilbanks will see you now. Please follow me," she said, leading him to a conference room at the end of the hall.

As Bill entered the room, he was met by a familiar face. Herman Moore was a longtime friend and client. Moore was an Aggie having graduated from Texas

A&M the same year Bill had finished Baylor. Shortly thereafter, they had met at a Dallas Chamber of Commerce get-acquainted mixer when both were in their mid-twenties.

"Good morning, Bill," said Herman Moore in his distinctive Texas drawl. "Meet our host, Clyde Wilbanks."

"My pleasure, Mr. Wilbanks," Bill said, extending his hand.

"Please, Bill. First names are in order today," the affable Triton Vice President responded with a firm handshake. "It's Clyde. And may I call you Bill?"

"Yes. Of course," Bill replied.

"Good. Glad you could set aside some time for us today," Wilbanks continued. "I think our discussions today will prove valuable when we have our sessions on Thursday in Athens."

In addition to Bill, Wilbanks, and Moore, one other person was in the conference room. "Meet Harry Spicer," Wilbanks gestured to the youthful, junior Triton executive standing next to Herman Moore.

"Good morning, Mr. Blevins," Spicer beamed, failing to heed the earlier announced protocol about using first names.

"Hello, Harry," Bill again extended his hand. "Good to meet you."

With introductions out of the way, the men settled into comfortable swiveled armchairs around an oversized, walnut-grained conference table and the meeting began. Wilbanks chaired the discussion but deferred to his younger colleague for the overview. Using a laptop that projected a PowerPoint presentation onto a ceiling-mounted screen, Harry Spicer detailed the objectives for the forthcoming trip to Athens. Bill and Herman Moore listened attentively and took notes.

According to Spicer, the supply chain issues were complicated by trade agreements, treaties, and bureaucratic red tape. The young man outlined an approach that addressed most of the matters but noted that the negotiations with the Israelis and their Greek shipping partners would need to take place when the group met in Athens. All four men seated around the table were planning to make the trip abroad.

Bill had gained a better understanding of the shipping issues but had not heard anything that shed light on his concerns about price discrepancies.

"Has anyone offered to explain why there is such a variance between prices listed in the Jaffa Industries' catalog and the prices Lone Star has been paying for parts?" Bill broached the subject that had been gnawing at him. His question was met with an uncomfortable silence.

Herman Moore was the first to speak. "Bill, is it possible we have been using an old catalog? Pricing for everything has increased dramatically since the COVID pandemic. Maybe it's as simple as that."

"The numbers just don't add up, Herman," Bill replied with more defensiveness in his voice than intended. "I have gone over every invoice for the past three years. From what I can tell, you are being ripped. Those prices and shipping fees are being padded and you need to know *why* and *by whom*."

"I'm not aware of any pricing irregularities," Wilbanks said. "But we can discuss that with the Jaffa Industries reps when we get to Athens. I think you will find everything in order. Jaffa has an impeccable reputation in the industry."

Bill made no further rebuttal but jotted a note to remind himself of this discussion when he met directly with the Israeli and Greek delegations.

# 7

# All Is Not Well

### Pecan Village – Thursday, June 9

"Has anyone made the coffee tonight?" Lance inquired as he laid his *Bible* and a few file folders on the reading table in the middle of the church's library. Built-in bookshelves lined the perimeter of the room, which was rarely used for its original purpose, but it made a good gathering place for small group meetings.

"Got you covered," answered Maurice Sherman, a prominent banker in Pecan Village and an elder at PVC. "It should be ready in five minutes."

The semi-monthly elders-staff meeting was a productive way for the leadership of the congregation to keep abreast of current issues and plan steps for future activities. Three elders served the church: Herbert Lampkin, an accountant for the local hospital; Maurice Sherman, the banker; and Myron Williams, one of the few African Americans residing in the community. He recently had been installed as superintendent of the Pecan Village Public Schools.

In addition to Lance, Joanne Bentley usually attended the meetings. The elders had hired her to serve as staff coordinator for children's classes and activities. Joanne graduated two years ago with a degree in Biblical Studies from Abilene Christian University. Her position at PVC was her first full-time job. She loved her work with the children, and it radiated in everything she did. Lance was especially pleased with her skills and the enthusiasm she brought to the office.

Gary and Beverly Potter were also in attendance this week. The couple's normal pattern was to stay only for the first segment of each meeting, a time when wellness reports and prayers were offered for those who were in hospitals or suffering at home from various illnesses. The Potters had organized a team of volunteers who made visits, provided meals, or rendered some service to those who were ailing. Although unpaid helpers, they were deemed valuable extensions of the church's staff.

"Let's stand and begin our meeting with prayer," Herbert Lampkin said, hardly waiting for everyone to rise before beginning his heartfelt plea. "Our Father God, bless our every thought and action tonight as we assemble in your Son's name. May we be honorable stewards of the trust You have demonstrated in us by placing these families at PVC into our care. Direct our steps tonight and always. In Jesus' name, amen." All took their seats except for Maurice who finished serving coffee to those who had asked for a cup.

Lance reviewed a list of members who needed prayers and visits. A teenage boy was in the hospital suffering injuries from an automobile crash. An elderly widow, who could no longer drive, needed help with grocery delivery and a ride to visit her doctor. There were others, but the list was short. The Potters wrote the names in a spiral notebook and assured the group that all needs would be addressed by their team members. Then, they excused themselves from the remainder of the meeting.

"Before we get into the other items on our agenda, Leonard England has asked for a few minutes of our time," Herbert announced. "Shall I have him come in?" A collective groan reverberated around the table.

"How many minutes is a few?" Lance asked with noticeable sarcasm in his voice.

"I told him we would carve out ten minutes, but no more," replied Herbert. "I'll try to hold him to that." He rose from his chair, walked to the door, and invited Leonard into the meeting.

Smiles and pleasantries were exchanged by all as the doddering old man entered the room. Lance extended his hand guardedly and said, "Good of you to come, Leonard."

Once seated, Herman inquired, "Leonard, you asked for a few minutes. What's on your mind?"

It was obvious to all that Leonard was distraught. He had not shaved in days and his hands were shaking as he sat slumped in his chair. "I don't raise objections often," Leonard began. He was the only one in the room who believed that preamble. "But I have heard just about all the grace 'mishmash' I can take. Does every sermon at this church have to pound grace into our heads? When is the last time we heard a lesson on *sin*? Or *heaven* and *hell*? Or *evangelism*?"

Lance was about to come out of his boots, but he lowered his head and bit his tongue. Tonight, this was not his fight. Either the elders had his back, or not. He had seen their resolve before and believed they would rise to the occasion once again.

Maurice Sherman was the first to respond. "Leonard, do you want to stand in Judgment before your Maker, relying only on what you have done in this life as payment for your salvation? Can any of us do enough to merit forgiveness for our sins and shortcomings? I, for one, am grateful for every sermon Lance preaches that reminds me of the grace that God has offered, and of the eternal hope that is mine because of his grace and mercy."

"I'm sorry," Leonard said softly. "But the sermons being preached today are nothing like the ones I remember hearing as a kid."

The room was quiet. The silence was broken only by a slight moan coming from Leonard. Gradually, the moan became a shallow sob as tears rolled down the older man's face.

"I don't know why I'm here tonight. Maybe I'm just getting too old. I feel like I'm standing in a line at the supermarket and I'm the next one ready to check out," Leonard mumbled.

Lance had a pang of compassion pour over him as he listened to a lonely old man who knew his remaining days on earth were few. He overcame his visceral reaction to Leonard's complaint and settled on a more comforting tone.

"Leonard, I'm not trying to preach lessons just like the ones someone preached fifty years ago," Lance said with kindness in his voice. "I love you like an elder brother, my friend, but my work is to preach lessons that are scripturally sound and that lead people to Jesus. If they include an abundance of grace, I pray we will accept the gift that God has given to all of us. It is central to our hope of salvation."

"I guess so," Leonard said in a barely audible voice. "Maybe I just need someone to pray with me."

A telephone rang outside the closed door. Joanne left the room to answer the call.

The elders encircled Leonard, praying for him that he might be consoled. His tears were flowing openly. The broken man appeared to treasure the loving attention and a new sense of belonging among his brethren. Lance assured him that he would begin a new adult Bible class to address some of the subjects Leonard felt were being neglected. It was a meaningful moment for all who were present.

Suddenly, the library door opened, and Joanne burst into the room in tears.

"It's all right, Joanne," Herbert reassured her. "We have had prayer and reconciliation with Leonard tonight. All is well."

"No!" she cried. "All is not well." Her voice was breaking, and her sobs became louder.

"The phone call was from Bill Blevins' son, Andy, in Dallas. His family was notified tonight that Bill was found dead in his hotel room in Athens. He was murdered!"

# 8

# Ministering Angels

**Pecan Village – Thursday, June 9**

A thousand thoughts flooded Lance's mind as he drove to the Blevins' home that night. Consoling a grieving family was never a pleasant assignment. The emotional pain was often raw, crippling, and expressed with little or no inhibition. Having come to realize that no two people grieve the same way, Lance had learned to take a careful assessment of each situation, listening more than talking, hoping to offer his best words of comfort for the moment.

As he pulled into the circular driveway and parked in front of the two-storied, stone house, he bowed his head, offering a silent prayer for divine guidance. *Lord, use me tonight as an instrument for good, for comfort, and for consolation. May the words of my mouth be a balm to the brokenhearted.*

Lance approached the front door, unsure whether to ring the doorbell or rap lightly on the door and walk inside. He chose the latter.

"Donna, it's Lance," he said reassuringly as he poked his head into the spacious living room. Two of the PVC elders, Maurice Sherman and Myron Williams, had arrived a few minutes before Lance. They were standing near a large, overstuffed sofa where a neighbor was seated next to Donna, holding her hand, and shedding tears with her friend.

"Oh, Lance. I don't know what to say," Donna exclaimed, reaching both arms upward to hug his neck. "I don't think I can bear this blow," she cried, barely able to get the words out of her mouth.

"There are no words for a time like this, Donna," Lance offered. "Tonight is a moment like none other in your lifetime."

He wanted to tell her, "*Let your tears flow and embrace the love your friends and neighbors shower upon you. Each one is an angel of God ministering to you as an expression of His love for you and your family.*" But for the moment, the less said was best.

"Lance, this is Susie Bowman," Donna looked toward her friend. "She and John live next door. I called them immediately after the sheriff came by the house. John is in Bill's study making some calls for me. I don't know what I would have done without them."

"Thank you, Susie, for being Donna's friend," Lance responded. "She will be leaning on you often over the next few months. I know the family is grateful for all you have done this evening to help her manage this dreadful news."

Susie bowed her head, hugging Donna tightly, and silently mouthed the words, "Thank you."

Looking toward Donna, Maurice said, "I know you have reached Andy because he was the one who called us at the church. Have you been able to reach Carla and Riley?"

"John was able to speak to all three," Donna said, her voice breaking as she thought of the unspeakable loss each child would experience without a father. "I tried but couldn't put two sentences together over the phone. All three children are planning to come sometime tomorrow."

Lance wanted to inquire about the details surrounding Bill's death but thought better about the timing. Whatever had happened would become known before long. Tonight needed to be devoted to Donna, her family, and the reality of their enormous loss.

John Bowman entered the room. "Donna, I was . . ." he interrupted himself as he noticed Lance. "John Bowman," he said, reaching for Lance's hand.

"Yes, John, so pleased to meet you. I'm Lance Arnold. Bill and Donna have been friends of mine for thirty years–ever since our law school days at Baylor. We worship together at Pecan Village Community Church near Travis Park," Lance explained. "It's good of you and Susie to be here tonight for Donna. Good neighbors are priceless."

"Wish there were more we could do, but this is anyone's worst nightmare," John said, turning toward Donna. "The sheriff's office has promised to call you as soon as they get additional information from the State Department or the authorities in Athens. I gave them my number in the event they were unable to reach you. By the way, Andy said he has decided to drive down from Dallas tonight. He expects to be here around three o'clock in the morning."

"Would you like for me to call Angie and have her spend the night, or at least stay until Andy arrives?" Lance offered, knowing that his wife would be willing to help Donna in any way she could.

"John and I will stay with her," Susie said. "We're right here and happy to do it." Donna dropped her head on Susie's shoulder and began to cry softly.

"Thank you, both," Lance said, glancing at John and Susie.

Then, he took a step toward Donna. "I cannot imagine the pain you feel, Donna, but I know you have a faith that will sustain you even in the darkest of times. Draw close to God tonight, closer than you have ever been before." He asked Myron Williams to lead them in prayer. After kissing Donna on the cheek, he left her in the care of the elders and her neighbors.

The drive home took Lance only a few minutes, but he crammed a week's worth of questions into his mind as he motored along the empty streets of Pecan Village. *How could something like this have happened? Was Bill's death accidental or was it, in fact, an intentional homicide? Could the Blevins family rely upon Greek authorities to resolve the criminal issues, or would there need to be some intervention from the U. S. State Department? How long would it take to have Bill's body returned to the States? What kind of funeral services would Donna choose, and would she want Lance to officiate?*

As he pulled into his driveway, Lance noticed a light shining through the master bedroom window. Angie was waiting for him and would expect him to share whatever he could about the tragic incident. She was always a good sounding board, and Lance had learned to rely on her intuitive judgments. Nothing about this matter was going to be easy to share, however, even with Angie.

# 9

# Not Much Here

**Athens – Thursday, June 9**

It was early Thursday afternoon in Athens, Greece. Inspector Giorgos Papadakis had been at his desk for two hours, poring over sketchy notes the crime scene inspectors had taken earlier that morning. An American attorney had been stabbed to death sometime before dawn in his Aristotle Hotel room. Inspector Papadakis looked again at the victim's name, *William G. Blevins from Pecan Village, Texas, USA.*

Blevins had arrived in Athens on Wednesday. From the airline voucher found in his suit jacket, local investigators had determined Blevins left New York's JFK Airport Tuesday evening on Delta Flight 262, arriving in Paris at the Charles de Gaulle Airport Wednesday morning. In Paris, he had transferred to Delta Flight 8683 which brought him to Athens early Wednesday afternoon. He had checked into the hotel at 3:12 p.m.

Three other Americans had made the trip with Blevins: Messrs. Clyde Wilbanks, Herman Moore, and

Harry Spicer. These men and three other persons of interest had been asked to meet with Inspector Papadakis at the police station Thursday afternoon. Appointments had been scheduled at thirty-minute intervals.

Sophia Baros, a junior member of the Athens' detective unit, approached Inspector Papadakis' desk. "We have Herman Moore waiting in the interrogation room," she said. "He is the one who knew the victim best. Are you ready to see him?"

"Give me five minutes, Sophia," Papadakis replied. He wanted to become more familiar with the thin dossier that had been hurriedly prepared on Herman Moore. Age fifty-five. Owner of Lone Star Electronics. A resident of Dallas, Texas. Married with two grown children. Had traveled to Athens frequently over the past five years. Business affiliations with Triton International, Jaffa Industries in Israel, and Maritime Shipping, Ltd., a British company operating out of Piraeus.

*Not much here*, Papadakis thought as he got up from his desk and made his way down the hallway. He was hopeful that Moore would be forthcoming with detail about Blevins' business activity in Athens and what he had been doing prior to the fatal incident. If nothing else, Moore might be able to provide information that would help the investigation find a motive for the murder. Without a motive, the inspector had found it was always more difficult to uncover legitimate suspects.

"Good afternoon, Mr. Moore," Papadakis greeted his guest while entering the small interrogation room. "I am Inspector Papadakis. You have met my associate, Inspector Baros. Sorry about your friend's death. We are fresh on the case and hope you can provide information that will enable us to gain some traction in this investigation."

"Thank you, inspector," Moore said, noticeably uncomfortable by the whole ordeal. "I'll be glad to cooperate anyway I can. Bill Blevins was a dear friend."

"I'm sure he was. Now, let's see, Mr. Moore, tell me the purpose of your trip. Why have you come to Athens?" the inspector probed.

Moore explained that Blevins was an attorney representing Lone Star Electronics and had agreed to accompany Moore and two executives with Triton International to resolve some shipping and pricing issues pertaining to electrical parts being manufactured in Israel. A two-day agenda included scheduled meetings with managers of Triton's Athens office, the Jaffa Industries representative who had flown to Greece from Tel Aviv, and a local official with Maritime Shipping.

"Were any of those meetings conducted Wednesday after your arrival?" Papadakis asked.

"No, not really. We met for dinner with some of the Triton staff Wednesday evening at the hotel, but the business meetings were all scheduled for today and, if more time was needed, we had agreed to meet tomorrow morning," Moore said.

"Who attended the Wednesday night dinner?" Sophia Baros broke into the discussion.

"Five of us had dinner in the Republic Dining Room last night. Bill Blevins and I, Clyde Wilbanks and Harry Spicer, who came with us from New York, and Alex Zerras, the manager of Triton's offices here in Athens," Moore replied. "We spent a little time discussing a few agenda items for Thursday's business meeting, but the evening was primarily a social event."

"Were any of you with Mr. Blevins after the dinner concluded?" Inspector Papadakis inquired.

"No, I don't think so. Bill excused himself early before any of us had ordered after-dinner drinks. He said that he needed to review some paperwork he had brought for our meetings," Moore answered. "As far as I know, he went directly to his hotel room."

"And why were the Jaffa Industries and Maritime Shipping reps not with you Wednesday night? Uh, let's see," the inspector looked down at his notes, "that would be, uh, Ms. Melamed and Mr. Jablonski. Were they invited to the dinner?"

"As I said, the dinner was purely social. The Triton boys from New York wanted to have some time to visit with Alex Zerras. He and Wilbanks used to work in the same office in New York. Our business sessions officially began this morning. Today was the first time I had the chance to meet Ms. Melamed and Mr. Jablonski," Moore replied.

The interrogation continued for another fifteen minutes, Papadakis and Baros digging for details and motives that might prompt someone to murder Blevins. Moore was candid in his answers, shedding light where he could, but unable to lead the investigators on a direct path toward any suspect.

"That's all for now," Inspector Papadakis said, as he stood, "Thank you for giving us this time, Mr. Moore. How long will you remain in Athens?"

"My return flight is on Monday. Am I clear to keep that schedule?"

"You're good to go. Travel well back to the States," the inspector said. "Here's my card. Naturally, we would appreciate any additional information you might recall that would be pertinent to the case."

Moore bid his farewells and walked out of the precinct station. If possible, he hoped to spend more time with Alex Zerras, pursuing some of the concerns Bill had raised about pricing and freight charges. He took a taxi back to the Aristotle Hotel.

"What's next, inspector?" Baros asked.

"Let's meet with the others and see if the stories are the same. I suspect they will be, but we don't have much to go on right now. Perhaps we can uncover a motive this afternoon. Also, I don't think we are dealing with a random killing. Blevins knew the person who killed him, or he wouldn't have let him enter his room. We need to pick up the thread that leads us to that person."

# 10

# Pack the Passports

**Pecan Village – Saturday, June 11**

Nothing had ever made a more shocking impact on the Pecan Village community than word of Bill Blevins' death. He was highly regarded by those who knew him, and his name was well respected by countless others. Bill's participation in various civic events was reported often in *The Eagle Banner*, the local weekly newspaper. In addition to his law practice, he had served as president of the public-school board, president of the local Rotary Club, and co-chairman with Donna for the annual arts festival. His death was deeply mourned in the small community.

The three Blevins children had arrived in Pecan Village to comfort their mother and assist with dozens of decisions that needed to be made in the ensuing days. Andy, the eldest, was the alpha male in the group. Now in his late twenties, he was married and had two sons. Having graduated from Southern Methodist University with a degree in finance, Andy was currently employed by Texas Instruments as an auditor in the treasurer's office.

His mother and siblings often deferred to his judgment whenever a family decision needed to be made.

Carla Whipple, also living in the Dallas area, had been a model child growing up in the Blevins' household. A straight "A" student. Valedictorian. A varsity cheerleader. Obedient, compliant, and eager to please. She was easy to love, and Bill and Donna loved her immensely. Carla had married the first boy she ever dated at SMU. Upon graduation, Daniel Whipple had gone to med school and had become a pediatrician in Plano, Texas. He and Carla had three children.

Riley Blevins was the baby brother that never grew up. He had been in and out of mischief since he was in junior high school. Bill had bailed him out of several scrapes with the law, but none that resulted in anything more than a fine and a deferred sentence. Currently, Riley was taking courses at Tarrant County College, hoping to secure a job that would allow him to be self-supporting. He was not married and showed no interest in finding a spouse.

Lance and Angie had been working feverishly to minister to the Blevins family since Thursday night's bombshell exploded. Angie, with help from the Potters, had arranged for food to be brought to Donna's home for at least the next week. Lance had invited the three elders to join him for a brief prayer session with Donna and the children. Both Lance and Angie had been on the telephone for hours, answering questions from parishioners and friends of the Blevins, and making calls to others who could be of some assistance to the family.

Taking a moment to catch their breath, Lance and Angie compared their respective "to-do lists" and ate a light lunch they had picked up at Benson's Deli.

"Do you have your sermon prepared for tomorrow?" Angie asked, knowing that Lance usually had his weekly lesson "in the can" well before Saturday.

"Yes and no," he replied. "I have the lesson I had prepared before hearing about Bill's death, but now I'm thinking I may need to go in a different direction. We'll see."

In the past, whenever tragedy had struck the church family, Lance had found himself feeling a need to address the universal question, "Why do horrible things happen to good people?" Sometimes he designed a sermon around the Old Testament character Job, while on other occasions he used the New Testament example of the Apostle Paul or of Jesus, himself. He did not pretend to have definitive answers to the issue but tried to show that God's involvement in human life had many more layers and complexities than mortals can fathom.

"Did I tell you that Andy wants to see me sometime this afternoon?" Lance said.

"No. Do you know what he wants?"

"Not for sure, but it may have something to do about a memorial service. I heard that Bill's body is being held in Athens until all the forensic work is completed by the Greek authorities. Not sure how long that will take."

"How's Donna doing?" Lance asked.

"About as you would expect," Angie replied. "She can't sleep and cries every time someone calls or drops by for a visit. The doctor has given her some medications, but the whole situation is extremely raw. There isn't much that anyone can do to ease the pain."

The telephone rang and Lance picked up immediately. "Hello. Yes, this is he. Oh, yes, hello. I just told Angie that you wanted to visit this afternoon. Now? Sure. Where do you want to meet? How about at the church building? We can use my office. I'm sure we can have some privacy there. Great. See you then."

"Andy?" Angie surmised.

"Yeah. I need to go. He wants to meet now while Donna is resting. I'm not sure how long this might take, but I'll call you if I'm going to be gone more than an hour or two." Lance picked up his paper plate and paper waste, tossing them in the kitchen trash can. He gave Angie a kiss on the cheek, grabbed his *Bible* and car keys, and hurried out the door.

The drive to the church building took Lance no more than ten minutes. When he arrived, he saw that Andy was already waiting for him in the parking lot. He was a handsome young man and reminded Lance of Bill's appearance during his student days at Baylor Law.

"Thanks, Mr. Arnold, for seeing me on short notice. The doctor gave Mom some sedatives and she has finally been able to sleep."

"No problem, Andy. Let's go inside. The building is always quiet on a Saturday afternoon. I'm sure we'll have the place to ourselves." Lance led the way through a side door that opened into a reception room adjacent to the minister's office.

"Do you care for a soft drink or coffee?" Lance offered.

"Would you have bottled water?"

"Coming right up. Have a seat on the sofa in my office. I'll be right there."

Andy was noticeably shaken about the events that had occurred the past forty-eight hours. He had hardly slept since hearing about his father's death and had been asking dozens of questions to anyone who would give him an audience. Lance was willing to listen and help wherever he could.

"Here you go," Lance said, handing a bottle of Evian to his visitor. "I can't imagine the nightmare you and your family are going through right now. Just let me know where I can help you the most."

For an hour, the men engaged in a free-wheeling exchange of thoughts and questions surrounding Bill Blevins' death. *Why did God allow this awful thing to happen? What lies beyond the grave? Will we know our loved ones in heaven? Why had the Greek government held up the return of Bill's body? What should the family do about a memorial service?*

"My wife and I have talked about it, Mr. Arnold." Andy's voice became stronger and more resolute. "With so many questions and so few answers, I am planning a trip to Athens. Lisa wants to go with me, but I've insisted that she not. She's five months pregnant, and an overseas flight is the last thing she needs right now."

"I understand why you feel the need to go, Andy, although I'm not sure what any of us can do right now," Lance said. "At the same time, I would want some straight answers from the authorities in Athens if I were in your shoes. You will need a U.S. Passport and a visa to enter Greece and obtaining the visa will take at least a week. I have some contacts, however, that may help expedite the process."

"I have a passport, but hadn't thought about needing a visa," Andy said. "Anything you can do along those lines would be appreciated."

"How would you feel about my going with you to Greece?" Lance gently probed. "I have a good friend who preaches for a church in Glyfada which is only a few miles from Athens. He might be useful in helping us get around the city."

"I couldn't ask you to do that Mr. Arnold . . .."

"Andy, it's Lance. Please call me Lance."

"Sure. Okay, uh, Lance. But I don't want to impose on you and Mrs. Arnold."

"You're not imposing. I have a current passport and have traveled to Greece a couple of times in the past five years. I can introduce you to some delicious baklava and my favorite sweet treat - coconut sticks sold by the street vendors."

Andy appeared delighted that Lance offered to go with him. He had limited experience in traveling abroad and Lance felt sure that he could be useful as another set of ears and eyes on the ground.

# 11

# Hotline Helper

**Athens – Sunday, June 12**

Giorgos Papadakis had lived alone in a two-story flat ever since his wife died in an automobile accident nine years ago. They had no children. In fact, he had no family living within 2500 kilometers of Athens. A stepbrother, Konstantinos Androsos, or Kostas as he was known to Giorgos, lived with his wife and three children in London. The two men had not seen each other in fifteen years and rarely communicated by phone or correspondence. Sadly, the inspector's social life was unimaginably dull.

Although his career in police work was an all-consuming element in his humble existence, Giorgos had Sundays off, and he relished having time to catch up with chores around his apartment unit. Today, he had decided to regrout some loose tiles in the bathroom shower and, if time permitted, change the oil in his 12-year-old Fiat. Since he was a teenager, he had always been good at repairing whatever needed to be fixed. It was a legacy left to him by his father.

The Sunday television news programs had been filled with stories and commentary about the gloomy state of the Greek economy. Inflation was out of control. Taxes were likely to go up the next time the Hellenic Parliament convened. On top of that, crime was on the rise in Athens and its suburban areas. *Is there nothing good to report today?* Giorgos thought as he finished eating a dish of homemade mutton stew.

After two hours of national broadcasting, a local television channel began to air news, weather, and sports reports regarding the happenings in Athens and nearby suburbs. A scandal involving the mayor was the lead story. Sexual harassment charges had been filed against Mayor Dimitrios Kalivas. He adamantly denied the allegations, but this was not the first time a woman had come forward claiming inappropriate advances by the seasoned politician. Shame constantly was associated with him and his office.

The newscaster's next story jolted Giorgos into full attention. "Athens police are investigating the apparent murder of an American businessman who was found dead in his room at the Aristotle Hotel Thursday morning. Currently, no suspects have been identified and no motive has been presented as a cause for the crime. The deceased, William G. Blevins, was an attorney from Texas and had been traveling with three business associates from the United States. Police Commissioner

Dinos Zervas reported Friday that he had assigned the case to his top investigative team and expected a quick resolution to the mystery surrounding the felonious attack."

*I'll consider that a pat on the back*, Giorgos smiled as he collected his dishes, placing them in the kitchen sink. Commissioner Zervas was known for being stingy with his compliments. "Top investigative team" might have been more of a tactic to keep reporters at bay than it was intended as kudos for Giorgos, but *whatever*. He turned off the television, tidied the kitchen, and went to his bedroom to take a Sunday afternoon nap.

Giorgos hardly had time to shut his eyes before the telephone rang. *No rest for the weary*, he thought as he picked up the receiver.

"Hello. Yes, it's me," the inspector said, not understanding why Sophia Baros could never recognize his voice even though she was calling him at home. "Yes, I saw the news story on television. Why? Is there something going on?"

Unlike Giorgos, Sophia worked on Sundays, choosing to take her day off in mid-week. She had taken a call at the precinct station that provided the inspectors with a new lead. According to the caller, after Bill Blevins left the dinner party Wednesday night, he met with someone else before retiring to his room. It was a fresh trail to pursue, and Sophia was eager to explore it.

"Sure, I can be there in about thirty or forty minutes," the inspector said. "I wonder why none of the Americans told us anything about his meeting *her*. Stay put, and I'll be right there."

Sophia had the name of a bellman who was working at the Aristotle Hotel Wednesday night and saw Blevins and a woman seated at the hotel's bar around 10:00 p.m. He had recognized Blevins from a photograph on the local television news report and had notified his hotel manager, who in turn had called the police hotline. These tips rarely produced new evidence, but in this case, it might lead the inspectors to the person who had last seen Blevins alive.

# # # # # #

The Aristotle was a brand-new hotel in Athens, located on Rovertou Galli Street in the central downtown district. Tourists loved to stay in the area as it was within easy walking distance of the Acropolis and other national monuments. Affiliated with Marriott Bonvoy's Loyalty Program, the Aristotle had become a popular choice with American businessmen. The boutique hotel offered a "fresh face" in a tired part of town.

Giorgos and Sophia arrived at the Aristotle at 3:45 p.m. and walked directly toward a young woman seated at the concierge's desk.

"We're here to see the hotel manager, uh," Giorgos hesitated as he reached for a slip of paper in his pocket. "Uh, . . . a Mr. Papko?" Both inspectors opened their police badges to identify themselves properly to the concierge. "He is expecting us."

"Yes, of course," the woman smiled. "Please follow me."

She rose from her desk and led the visitors across the lobby to an imposing mahogany door located behind the guest reception station. Opening the door, she invited Giorgos and Sophia to follow her to a corner office suite where Andreas Papko and his executive team managed the hotel's business affairs.

Papko, a stocky, bald man in his fifties, was seated behind his desk. His door was ajar. The concierge tapped lightly on the door frame.

"Mr. Papko, you have guests from the Athens Police Department," she announced.

The hotel manager looked up from his paperwork, dismissed the concierge, closed the door, and invited the inspectors to be seated in chairs across from his desk.

"Thank you for seeing us on such short notice," Giorgos began. "We're here investigating the murder . . ."

"Yes. Yes. I know why you are here, inspector. The police have been in and out of the hotel for the past three days. I'm surprised we haven't already met."

Giorgos collected his thoughts and began again. "I understand one of your employees may have seen the murder victim, Mr. Blevins, and perhaps another person late Wednesday evening at the hotel's bar?"

"Yes. Yes. That's correct, or at least that's what Dimitri says," Papko confirmed.

"Would we be able to visit with him this afternoon?"

"Yes. Yes. He is one of our bellmen and is currently on duty. I told him you were coming and that you would want to speak with him. Our conference room is open. Shall I have him meet you there?"

"Please. Truly kind of you." Giorgos was hopeful this was the lead that would help the inspectors break open the case.

# 12

# Mystery Woman

**Athens – Sunday, June 12**

Giorgos and Sophia waited patiently for Dimitri Venito to join them in the executive suite's conference room. Beneath a well-practiced, professional composure, each inspector was slightly on edge, hoping that this new witness might offer the information they needed. They knew better than to get their hopes high lest it became a lead, like many others, which went nowhere. But a thorough investigation into all leads and evidence was their job. It was how criminal cases were solved and both investigators were good at their jobs.

A rap on the door broke the room's silence. "Come in," Giorgos said.

Andreas Papko opened the door and led a young man, dressed in a navy blue, gold-trimmed bellman's suit, into the room. "Inspectors Papadakis and Baros, meet Dimitri Venito, our night bellman at the Aristotle."

Venito was a tall, slender young man in his late twenties. He had black, wavy hair and wore dark-rimmed eyeglasses. "*Kalispera*," the young man said, shaking hands with the inspectors. The greeting was Greek, but the accent was most definitely Italian.

"Please, have a seat, Mr. Venito," the inspector said, gesturing to a chair across the table from Sophia.

"If you need anything more from me, inspector, I'll be back in my office," Papko said as he exited the room, closing the door behind him.

A pregnant silence filled the room for a moment before Giorgos broke its spell. "Thank you for meeting with us this afternoon, Mr. Venito. You don't mind if we ask a few questions?"

"No, sir," the young man replied.

"How long have you been employed at the Aristotle, Mr. Venito?"

"Three years, sir."

"Always as a bellman?"

"Well, I began as a busboy in the Republic Dining Room," he said, "but moved to the bell stand about two years ago."

"Do you like working at the hotel, Mr. Venito?"

"Yes sir, it's okay. They don't pay me much, but the tips are good. It's a job. It's okay."

Giorgos always took some initial warmup pitches when interrogating a witness, hoping to obtain a better feel for the person's general demeanor and to put him or her more at ease. He decided it was time to get the main issue on the table.

"Mr. Venito, I understand that you may have seen William Blevins a few hours before he was murdered last week. Is that correct?"

"Yes, sir."

"How can you be sure that the person you saw was Mr. Blevins?"

"Because I was the one who carried his luggage to his room Wednesday afternoon when he checked into the hotel. He gave me a very generous tip. Ten thousand drachma. Same man. Same name. I won't forget him."

"Where was Mr. Blevins when you saw him Wednesday night?"

"He was seated in a booth in the Olive Branch Lounge."

"Can you tell us what you remember about that occasion, Mr. Venito?"

Venito looked down at his hands for a moment and then slowly raised his head, looking directly at the inspectors. "I had gone to the bar to get some water for a lady who had just arrived at the hotel. She was having a coughing spell that wouldn't stop. I offered to get her a bottle of water. I went to the Olive Branch and that's when I saw the American. He was having drinks with a woman who was also a guest at the hotel," he said.

"She was a guest at the hotel? Are you sure she was staying at the Aristotle?"

"Yes sir. I also carried her luggage to her room the day before the American arrived."

"And her name?" the inspector asked his cooperative witness.

"I'm not at liberty to share names, Mr. Inspector, but you may want to ask Mr. Papko. He knows her name."

Giorgos shot a glance at Sophia. She nodded, excused herself, and left the conference room. The inspector turned his attention back to Venito.

"Can you describe this woman for me? What did she look like, Mr. Venito? Was she tall? Short? Anything at all that you can remember."

"Well, I would say she was about five feet five or six inches tall, medium build. She had dark hair. I would guess that she was in her late twenties, maybe early thirties."

"Can you describe her clothing or anything special about her appearance?"

"I can't recall exactly what she wore . . . a dark-colored dress, I think."

"Would you be able to identify this woman if you saw her again?"

"Oh, yes! For sure," the bellman affirmed.

Giorgos was certain Venito would be a credible witness to establish that Blevins had met someone at the Olive Branch Lounge, but that would not place the mystery woman at the crime scene.

"Do you recall if Mr. Blevins appeared to be afraid or angry when talking to this woman? Was there any outward display of emotion?"

"None that I could tell. I think they were looking at some papers on the table, but I can't be sure about that."

"Was there anyone else engaged in conversation with Mr. Blevins and the woman that evening? Are you aware of anyone who might have gone with him to his room?"

"No, sir. That was the last time I saw Mr. Blevins. It was somewhere around 10:00 p.m. My shift is over at ten and I was getting ready to call it a day."

"Thank you, Mr. Venito," Giorgos said as he rose to his feet. "You have been extremely helpful. I think that will take care of everything for now."

"Glad to help," the Italian said.

He made his way to the door, almost bumping into Sophia as she burst into the room. She apologized for her awkward entrance, bid Venito farewell, closed the door, and turned to Giorgos. "I've got it. Papko gave me the woman's name."

# 13

# Cartel Conspiracy

**Jaffa and Piraeus – Tuesday, June 7**

Although scarred by her abandonment as a child, Leah Melamed had made the best of the unfortunate circumstances of her past. Upon graduating from high school, she was happy to be offered a job as a shipping clerk at Jaffa Industries. The position suited her skills-set, and the paycheck made her feel like a productive adult.

Leah continued to live with her grandmother until she came home from work one afternoon and found "Beebe" lying dead on the kitchen floor. Miriam Steinmann had died of a heart attack on Leah's twenty-fourth birthday. Rachel Braun, Leah's aunt, was the only family member Leah could turn to for comfort and assistance with decisions in handling Miriam's estate.

Trained by Yosef Cohen, the youthful shipping manager at Jaffa Industries, Leah was promoted from her entry-level position to assistant shipping manager in a matter of three years. There was a period when Yosef appeared to have had a romantic interest in her, but the relationship had not matured. More than once, the thought had crossed her mind that the brief courtship with her handsome young boss had merely been an exercise to groom her, fraught with ulterior motives.

Four years after her first promotion, Leah became the manager in charge of the entire shipping operations. She was a rising star at Jaffa. Yosef returned to the executive suite working alongside Ishmael Reuben, the company's Executive Vice President of Operations. He visited with Leah monthly when he brought her an envelope filled with cash that was equivalent to her regular paycheck.

On the surface, Jaffa Industries was a highly respected organization, marketing its products internationally and growing its net worth annually. It had almost cornered the market on a select number of electronic components that were used extensively in computerized manufacturing equipment. The company's research and development team far outpaced any of its competitors.

That was how business at Jaffa Industries appeared to operate on the surface. Unknown to all but a few was the underbelly of the enterprise. Aware that shipments were being sent to cities throughout the world, a few felonious executives had found a way to form a cartel, dealing in drugs and laundering money by using the company's normal course of commerce. Drugs were smuggled out of Jaffa to Piraeus, Greece, hidden alongside the regular orders being sent to Jaffa's customers. In Piraeus, accomplices at Maritime Shipping intercepted the packages and removed the drugs for distribution through local carriers. After taking the excess shipping fees hidden in each outgoing invoice for themselves, the Maritime team sent payments back to the Jaffa Cartel for a fresh supply of drugs.

Packing the smuggled goods in secret cavities within the shipping containers, and thereby hiding them from discovery by port authority officials, took exceptional skills and tedious attention to detail. Leah Melamed had been recruited by the cartel to handle this indispensable role. She, working long hours undercover with a small team from Jaffa's shipping department, produced enormous returns for their fellow conspirators. All were paid handsomely for their efforts.

When word was received that Triton International officials wanted to meet in Athens with representatives of Jaffa Industries to discuss shipping issues raised by Lone Star Electronics, a red alert was sounded within the cartel. A covert meeting was held in the home of one of the cartel bosses. It was decided that Leah needed to be sent to Athens as Jaffa Industries' representative and that her counterpart with Maritime Shipping should also participate in the discussions. The supply chain of drugs and laundered money between Jaffa and Piraeus had to be protected at all costs.

Leah was aware of what was expected of her by the cartel. Not only was the illicit gravy train at risk, but the discovery of any criminal behavior would surely result in prison terms for all persons involved. She was instructed to fly to Athens two days before Thursday's scheduled appointment with the Triton executives, link up with Aleksy Jablonski, her Maritime counterpart and a cartel accomplice, and for the two of them to devise a plan that would *permanently resolve* the cartel's concerns.

On Tuesday morning, Leah left Ben Gurion Airport in Tel Aviv aboard an Aegean Airlines flight bound for Greece. Upon arrival in Athens, she rolled a carry-on bag through the airport corridors and began her search for Aleksy. The Pole was a brute of a man who should be easy to spot in a crowd. Her impression of Aleksy had always been that he was not the type of person you would wish to meet in a dark alley.

Aleksy had made a new life for himself since moving from Poland to Piraeus, the large port city near Athens. He had worked hard, first as a stevedore and then as a foreman, before ascending to his current post, a superintendent of transport operations. Those employees who worked closely with Aleksy found him to be a no-nonsense boss who was a gifted multi-tasker. He could keep more plates spinning in the air than a juggler performing at the circus.

The truth be told, Aleksy made effective use of his juggling skills. He was, in fact, living a double life. By day, he managed his workers at Maritime, and at night he sent scores of drug peddlers into the streets of Athens.

The Pole had been recruited almost ten years ago by the conspirators of the Jaffa Cartel and had become a lynchpin in their drug and money laundering operations at Piraeus. Along the way, the former leader of the Green Wasps had become surprisingly wealthy.

Leah, who had worked closely with Aleksy over the past three years, identified her contact waiting by the taxi stand outside the airport. After making the short walk to the parking garage, he drove her to Piraeus, a few kilometers southwest of Athens. They ate lunch at a small bistro where the two collaborators began assessing the facts of Lone Star Electronics' contentions as they knew them. They had twenty-four hours to come up with a plan.

"From what I have been told, the one who is making the loudest noise is the lawyer from Texas," Aleksy said. He had worked with Leah long enough to trust her with the most sensitive information. Without question, they were members of the same team.

"How much do you think he knows about our arrangement?" Leah asked, looking directly into Aleksy's cold, green eyes.

"Not sure. He's been making noise about the difference between your catalog prices and the costs shown on his invoices. I know that for certain. And he wants your products sent directly to the States. How's that going to work for us? I also know this: if he digs deeply enough into the pricing, he may hit a mine that will blow us all out of the water. We must shut down this alarm."

"Shut down?"

"Yes. I mean *shut down*!"

Leah stirred cream and sugar into a fresh cup of coffee and took a sip. She did not like the way this conversation was going but agreed that the American's probing into any cost discrepancies was a big problem. They visited for another hour before Aleksy took Leah back to Athens where she checked into the Aristotle Hotel.

# 14

# See You in the Morning

**Athens – Wednesday, June 8**

Once he had settled into his room at the Aristotle Hotel, Bill made a brief list of items he needed to handle before having dinner with his business colleagues. A telephone call to Donna was at the top of the list. He rarely went anywhere without checking in at home.

The time differential between Athens and Pecan Village was eight hours. He decided to call Donna at 5:00 p.m. which would be 9:00 a.m. in Texas. She had grown accustomed to his being away on business trips, but it was reassuring for her to hear his voice and to know he had made the trip safely.

"Hello, dear. Just made it to the hotel in Athens. Wish you were here with me," Bill said.

"Hi, darling. I wish I were there too, but glad you made it safe and sound."

"You would love the Aristotle Hotel and its location. The Acropolis and museums are only a block or two away."

They spent a few minutes sharing stories about the grandchildren. Both were enjoying their new grandparenting roles, Donna as "Mimi" and Bill as "Papa Bear." Their cell phones were loaded with pictures and videos of the grands. They could never get enough news about the busy little bees and their adventures.

"Are you feeling okay?" Donna changed the subject, sensing tiredness in his voice.

"Just a little road weary, but I got some sleep on the flight to Paris. I'm fine."

"When do your meetings begin?" Donna asked.

"Dinner is the only thing on tap tonight. Purely social. Our business discussions begin in the morning."

"Okay. Get some rest tonight and call me tomorrow. I love you."

"Love you too," Bill said and ended the call.

Needing to freshen up after a full day of air travel, Bill stepped into a warm shower and spent the next ten minutes allowing the pulsating spray to massage his aching body. After one round of shampoo, shower gel, and rinsing, he went through the whole cycle again.

A brief nap was the next item on Bill's list. He slipped into his underwear, set a one-hour alarm on his cell phone, and pulled back the covers on the king-sized bed. Before he was able to lie down, however, he noticed that an envelope had been slipped beneath his door. He stooped down and picked up the ivory envelope, fashionably marked with the Aristotle Hotel logo. On the outside of the envelope, the name *William G. Blevins* was scrawled in black ink. He tore away the sealed flap, pulled out a handwritten note, and read it.

*"Welcome to Athens, Mr. Blevins. I look forward to meeting you later this evening. If I may, I would like to ask a favor. When Clyde Wilbanks set up our agenda, he did not include the representatives of Jaffa Industries or Maritime Shipping for tonight's dinner. Leah Melamed arrived Tuesday and has told me that she has some information that may be helpful regarding your concerns over the invoice cost discrepancies. You may want to call her before our business session in the morning. She is staying at the Aristotle in room 410. Thank you, Alex Zerras."*

Although Bill had never met Zerras, he knew who he was. Triton's European headquarters was in Athens and Zerras had been the division's chief officer for the past eight years. He had a reputation for being a tough-talking, hard-driving executive who rarely met anyone his equal. Taking the note at face value, Bill decided to call Ms. Melamed and see if they could meet sometime after his dinner concluded. Once he had set a time and place with her, he could finally get down for a nap.

# # # # # #

Alex Zerras hosted the small dinner party in a private alcove that was part of the Republic Dining Room, the Aristotle's premier restaurant. Bill sat next to Herman Moore on one side of the table, Clyde Wilbanks and Harry Spicer sat across from them, and Zerras commanded the end of the table. He had preordered a rack of lamb as the entrée for himself and his four guests. Bill blanched when he saw it. He hated lamb.

The conversation around the table covered many subjects, but none that pertained directly to the sessions planned for tomorrow. Zerras shed some light on the dismal economic news that was pushing Greece into an unwelcomed recession. Harry Spicer had never been to Athens and asked for suggestions on touring the sites. Herman and Bill entertained the group with Texas-style braggadocio and stories regarding their favorite football teams, the Texas A&M Aggies and the Baylor Bears. It was a congenial group, sparring gently with one another in anticipation of the business that brought them together in this city of antiquities.

Once his guests had finished dinner, Zerras suggested they order drinks to cap off the night. Bill used the break as his opportunity to bid the group farewell and keep his appointment with Leah Melamed.

"If you will excuse me, I need to handle a matter or two before the evening is over," Bill said, rising from the table. "I've enjoyed the conversation and the good company. Thank you, Alex, for an excellent dinner. I'll see all of you in the morning."

The Olive Branch Lounge was on street level, one floor below the Republic. Bill took the stairs and made his way to the cash register stand at the lounge's circular bar. It was there he had agreed to meet the Israeli woman with whom he could discuss Jaffa Industries' catalog pricing and shipping practices. If the issues could be settled, this woman had a role to play in his client and Jaffa's coming to an equitable solution.

# 15

# The Olive Branch

**Athens – Wednesday, June 8**

Bill and Leah had agreed to meet at the Olive Branch Lounge at 9:00 p.m. or shortly thereafter. He had allowed some wiggle room in the event he was unable to excuse himself from the dinner party with Herman Moore and the men from Triton. As he entered the lounge, he glanced at his watch. *Three minutes after nine*. His earlier calculation to set the time for their meeting had proven to be right on target.

*But where was Leah Melamed*? The only women in the room were seated with men and fully engaged in conversation. Surveying the lounge, he saw no single female standing at the bar, seated at the tables, or occupying any of the booths that lined two sides of the room. He moved closer to the cashier's stand at the bar and waited for his Israeli contact to arrive.

At fifteen minutes after the hour, a dark-haired woman in her late twenties walked into the Olive Branch, paused for a moment to scan the room, and smiled when she caught Bill's eye. She approached the American with a stride that oozed self-confidence. Bill had little doubt that he was about to meet a formidable adversary.

"You must be Mr. Blevins," Leah said as she offered her hand. Her Middle Eastern accent was noticeable, but not difficult to understand.

"Yes, but please, call me Bill. And do you mind if I call you Leah?"

"Of course not. Bill and Leah," she said, nodding her head in approval. "How was your trip from the States?"

It was the normal question that always allowed a visitor to tell of his traumatic experiences while flying internationally. A snafu here, a weather delay there, or an obnoxious passenger's spat with an airline flight attendant. There were always stories to be told about commercial flying, and they usually helped two strangers find common ground.

"Not much to tell. We had a little turbulence over the Atlantic on our way out of New York, but it cleared. The rest of the trip was smooth sailing."

Leah was much younger than Bill had surmised and far more attractive. Her dress, although not necessarily provocative, was cut low in the front and short at the hemline. Wanting to be a gentleman, he tried not to notice but occasionally caught himself losing eye contact.

"Shall we take one of the booths?" Bill suggested. "It may give us room to look at a few papers I've brought along." The booth did give them some working space and additional privacy. They sat across from one another as if ready for the first pawn to be moved on the chessboard.

"May I buy you a drink?" Bill offered. Personally, he was not big into "adult beverages." He would occasionally have a mimosa at a reception, and on rare occasions, a glass of wine with a meal or a beer with the boys at Lone Spur's grill after a round of golf, but he had no taste for hard liquor. His Baptist upbringing still tempered his judgment on drinking. Leah ordered a Perrier with a slice of lime.

"You are aware that my client, Lone Star Electronics, is a significant buyer of goods from your company," Bill began. "Last year, they purchased more than $8 million in parts and equipment from Jaffa Industries."

"Yes, I understand they have been a very good customer of ours for several years. We value our relationship with Lone Star and with Triton."

"Well, here's the problem. Mr. Moore is unhappy that shipments of his goods to Dallas are being channeled through Athens and New York City before being sent to Texas. In our meetings tomorrow, we will be asking for direct service from Tel Aviv to Dallas. Will that be a problem?" Bill studied Leah's face for any hint of resistance. She was expressionless.

"Those matters are not as easily handled as they may appear. Trade treaties and shipping contracts tie our hands, but we can look into your request and see what can be done."

"Good," Bill said. "I know Herman Moore would be pleased if you can act favorably on this issue. If you do, I would like to think he would see some savings in those exorbitant freight costs he has been paying."

He paused a moment before raising the more delicate question. "One more thing. Are you able to explain why Jaffa's catalog pricing is so different from invoices being paid by Lone Star? As we say in Texas, *something about this operation doesn't pass the smell test.*"

Leah had anticipated his question. It was the reason she had flown to Athens. Nonetheless, it was a question that could only be answered with lies and subterfuge. Reluctantly, and a bit defensively, she waded in.

"I don't understand," she said. "Are you suggesting that my company is being dishonest with your client? Really, Bill, I resent that insinuation."

"Leah, I have brought copies of invoices–a dozen or more–that illustrate major discrepancies between catalog and invoice pricing. Look for yourself. Here are the last two invoices with a breakout of prices being charged to Lone Star. And here is the current catalog. I have circled in red the corresponding items from the invoice."

He paused only a second, not giving Leah a chance to respond. Then, he placed on the table the matter that gave him the most concern. "Furthermore, I have some inkling that the first issue about shipping may be related to the second issue on pricing."

There it was! Leah had heard it straight from the American's mouth. He was on the trail that could upend the cartel's entire drug and money laundering operation. Aleksy was right. One way or another, this American attorney's fishing expedition needed to be *shut down*.

Trying not to overreact, Leah lowered her voice and looked directly into Bill's eyes. "Mr. Blevins, I have a file folder in my room that will explain everything you seek to know about Jaffa's pricing and shipping practices. Give me fifteen minutes and I will drop the folder by your room so that you can study the material before tomorrow's meeting."

"Why not just walk me through it now?" Bill quizzed his sparring mate.

"It is material that is better read than talked about. Look at the information in the file folder and I am sure you will find answers to your questions. If I tried to walk you through the trade agreements and shipping contracts without that folder, I would only confuse us both."

"All right," Bill conceded. "I'm in room 310. Drop the folder off at my room within the next fifteen minutes. I'm feeling a little jetlagged and need to get down for some sleep or I won't be able to function tomorrow."

"I'll be there as quickly as I can."

# 16

# Shut Down

**Athens – Wednesday, June 8**

Bill returned to his room with an uncomfortable feeling in his stomach. Leah Melamed was a jig-saw puzzle in high heels. On the one hand, she was cordial and cooperative, trying to assist in solving Lone Star's shipping delays. At the same time, she offered no solution for the troublesome discrepancy that existed between Jaffa's invoices and its catalog prices. And when Bill had linked the first matter of concern with the second – *Whoa*! Her tone had become totally different. He revisited the conversation in his mind. *I was no longer Bill. I became Mr. Blevins!*

Bill's hotel room was a mess. He had left an open suitcase on the bed, paperwork and file folders stacked on the credenza, dirty clothes on the floor near the closet, and damp linens scattered all over the bathroom floor. Shifting his forward gear into overdrive, he made the room as tidy as it had been when he first arrived. He was about to have company.

Even for a man with Bill's moral principles, the thought of having an attractive young woman come to his hotel room, late at night, was titillating. He loved Donna and believed with all his heart in the sanctity of marriage. Marital fidelity was embedded in his DNA. Nonetheless, he wrestled in his mind whether he should invite Leah into his room or simply take the folders from her when he opened the door. He had not had time to work through the dilemma when he heard a knock on the door.

"Coming," Bill said, checking the room once again to be sure it looked presentable for his guest. Upon opening the door, he saw Leah, frowning slightly and holding a manila folder in both hands.

"Would you like to . . .," Bill stopped in mid-sentence when he saw a massive form push Leah aside and barge into the room, slamming Bill to the floor as he entered.

Aleksy Jablonski had been hiding against a wall in the hallway when Leah knocked on Bill's door. She was the appetizer. The Pole was the main course. Once the door was opened, Aleksy used the element of surprise to take Bill down with a bruising tackle that would have made any NFL defensive coach give his linebacker a high five.

Before Bill could collect his senses and rally to his defense, Aleksy had used a lead pipe to crack his victim's skull. He struck Bill across the head three times, rendering him unconscious, and then pulled an eight-inch dagger from a sheath hidden inside Aleksy's coat. Showing no mercy, he plunged the dagger deep into Bill's chest, just below the sternum, repeating the murderous blows seven or eight times. For good measure, Aleksy used the dagger to slit Bill's throat, severing the carotid artery. In less than a minute, the vile deed was done. Any threat to the Jaffa Cartel had been *shut down.*

Leah had stayed just long enough to witness the initial blows with the pipe. The moment Aleksy plunged the dagger into Bill's chest, she had run down the hall and taken the stairwell up to her room on the fourth floor. There she bolted the door, threw herself on the bed, and began to cry uncontrollably. *Surely there was some other way to have silenced the American*, but Aleksy had insisted that he would take care of the problem and he had. Her superiors in Jaffa would be pleased with the result.

# # # # # #

The Odysseus Room at the Aristotle was a comfortable setting for any small group meeting. Guests were always captivated by the remarkable view from its balcony. The iconic Parthenon, in all its glory, sat atop Acropolis Hill as if it were a sculpted appendage to the hotel. Alex Zerras had booked the room as a meeting place for business discussions with his American colleagues and others whom they had invited to participate. The first session was scheduled to begin Thursday morning at nine o'clock sharp.

Zerras had arrived early at the hotel to be certain all arrangements were in order. Clyde Wilbanks and Harry Spicer were the first Americans to find the room and they exchanged warm greetings with their host. Wilbanks and Zerras had been with Triton for more than twenty years, working together in New York before Zerras landed the executive position in Athens. The two men swapped a few "remember when" stories, much to young Spicer's amusement.

Next to appear were Leah Melamed and Aleksy Jablonski. Zerras was acquainted with Aleksy, having done business with Maritime Shipping for years, but it was his first time to meet Leah. Introductions were exchanged, followed by small talk while the group waited for Herman Moore and Bill Blevins to arrive.

At ten minutes after the hour, Herman Moore peeked in the door.

"Am I at the right place?" he said, trying to spot a familiar face.

"You found us, Herman," Wilbanks replied. "Better late than never."

"I guess that jetlag got the best of me. I hit the sack early last night and slept through my morning alarm. My apologies."

Wilbanks introduced Moore to Leah and Aleksy and then asked, "Have you seen Bill?"

"Not since dinner last night," Moore replied. "Should I give him a ring?"

"It's up to you. He's your attorney. Do you think we need to wait?"

"Not really," Moore said. "He'll be here shortly. He can catch up on our discussions once he arrives."

With that item settled, the meeting began. Wilbanks had prepared the agenda for the morning and chaired the discussion from his end of the conference table. They had barely had time for Wilbanks' review of how the six parties at the table were intertwined in various business transactions when they heard a knock at the door. Andreas Papko, the Aristotle Hotel manager, poked his head into the room and asked if he could speak privately with Zerras. The men conferred quietly in the hallway for a few minutes.

When Zerras returned, he said solemnly, "I have some terrible news. Bill Blevins was found dead in his room this morning by a housekeeper. He was murdered sometime last night."

# 17

# Sunset on Mars Hill

### Athens – Thursday, June 23

American Airlines flight 6848 was making its final approach to Athens International Airport for an on-time arrival at 5:55 p.m. EET. Andy and Lance had boarded fifteen hours ago in Dallas, made a short layover stop at London Heathrow, and were more than ready to get their swollen feet on the ground. Andy had hardly slept on the plane. Except for some long weekends spent in the Caribbean, the trip to Greece was his first time traveling abroad.

"There it is," Lance said, pointing toward the Parthenon atop Acropolis Hill. "Nothing quite like it, unless you count replicas like the one in Nashville."

"Stunning, for sure," Andy replied, unable to take his eyes off the international landmark. "I hope we can find time to walk around the area while we're here. I promised Lisa some pictures."

Two weeks had passed since Pecan Village residents had learned of Bill Blevins' murder in Athens. The family had received an outpouring of condolences from their many friends and from people they hardly knew, but no expression of comfort could bring a slain husband and father home. They were not prepared for the finality of Bill's passing, nor for the haunting reminder of the tortuous way he had been murdered. The ordeal had been a relentless nightmare.

The U. S. State Department had made several overtures to its counterpart in Greece, asking for Bill's body to be returned to Texas. To date, those requests had not been honored with a favorable reply. The coroner who had been assigned to the case and the Athens Police Department's forensic division had been overly cautious about releasing the corpse until satisfied nothing more was to be gained for the investigation by keeping it. The delay had been especially painful for the family.

Andy and his sister Carla had decided to remain a few weeks in Pecan Village, staying with Donna for her comfort and emotional support. Riley, hesitant to miss more of his classes at Tarrant County College, had gone back to the metroplex. The date for a Bill Blevins memorial service was still pending.

Following up on Andy and Lance's earlier conversation about making a trip to Athens, Lance had set some wheels in motion. He placed a call to Shane Lawson, a former law school buddy who currently led the legal department for Exxon in Houston, and asked a favor. One week later, tourist visas arrived for Lance and Andy.

Lance had also placed a call to Nico Panagos, his friend who preached for the church in Glyfada, Greece. In addition to his ministerial duties, Nico, a native Greek, was a licensed national tour guide who often took Christian groups to visit the Grecian historic sites that were referenced in the *Bible*. Three years ago, Lance had been a tourist on one of his excursions. Nico was happy to hear from Lance and promised to meet his plane when he and Andy arrived in Athens.

From a crowded carousel of overstuffed duffels, backpacks, and suitcases, the two Texans found their luggage and made their way to the Hertz shuttle station outside the airport's front doors. There stood Nico wearing a sporty Greek fishing hat and carrying a sign that read, *Welcome Lance and Andy*. His smile also said, *welcome*!

It was a bittersweet moment. Nico was happy to renew his acquaintance with Lance, but the reason for his trip to Athens was painfully sad. Lance facilitated the introductions for Andy and Nico, telling each what he admired about the other. Nico offered his heartfelt sympathy to Andy over the passing of his father. Then, the three men, sharing a bond of brotherhood through their faith and the mission that had brought them together, made their way to the parking garage. After cramming themselves and their luggage into Nico's five-year-old Toyota Yaris, they were off.

"I have a surprise for you," said Nico. "You have arrived just in time to watch the sunset on Mars Hill. I know you're tired, but it's a glorious moment that I must share with you. Can we do it?" He knew the Americans were exhausted from their trip, but the best way to keep them from suffering jetlag over the next few days was to be sure they did not go to bed too early tonight.

"Sure, why not?" Lance said. "How about you, Andy?"

"I'd love to see Mars Hill. Tonight's good by me."

"Great!" Nico said. "We'll drop your bags and the car off at the hotel, grab a bite to eat, and walk to Acropolis Hill. They light up the Parthenon when it begins to get dark. You're going to love it."

The Americans, luggage in hand, registered for their rooms at the front desk of the Aristotle Hotel while Nico had his car valeted to a nearby parking garage. Although fatigued, Andy and Lance found their second wind and were ready for a new adventure. The day might have been long, but the night was young. With Nico in the lead, they walked to a nearby café where their Greek travel companion ordered three gyros to go.

Mars Hill, better known to the locals as the Areopagus, was a short walk from the café. The rock outcroppings immediately northwest of the Parthenon were unimpressive in themselves, but its history and the view from its meandering trails more than compensated for its indiscriminate form. Nico led his guests to his favorite resting spot and told them about the area's ancient past.

"Areopagus simply means, 'the hill of Ares,' named for Ares, the Greek god of war. It became known as *Mars Hill* under the Romans whose god of war was Mars. The term can refer either to this physical site or to an ancient body of Athenian elders who acted initially as a governing body. Later, the group became a judicial court, hearing homicide cases somewhere in the vicinity of these rocks where we stand tonight."

"Incredible," Andy said in amazement. "Greek history goes back centuries upon centuries. It makes American history seem so recent and shallow."

"I could tell you so much more, but let's eat a bite here and watch the sunset," Nico said. "They should be turning the lights on at the Parthenon before long."

"Excellent!" said Andy, taking a big bite of his sandwich. "What a view."

"Nico, when I came here three years ago, you read some of the Apostle Paul's words from his sermon on Mars Hill. Would you do that for Andy and me tonight?" Lance implored.

"Of course. I'd be honored." Nico pulled from his pocket a small New Testament and turned to the seventeenth chapter of Acts. He began with the twenty-second verse and read to the end of the chapter. " . . . the God who made the world and all things in it, since He is Lord of heaven and earth, does not dwell in temples made with hands . . ." He had read the passage many times to visitors from all over the world, but he never tired of hearing Paul's message.

"Look," cried Andy, "the sun is about to set." Nico was right. The sunset seen from Mars Hill was a spectacular sight. The young men silently embraced the moment as if it were the prelude to the Second Coming of the Lord.

A few seconds later, the outdoor floodlights bathed the Parthenon in a marvelous display of light and shadow. "What a memory-maker," Andy exclaimed as he pointed his cell phone toward Acropolis Hill and began shooting a video to show Lisa.

The magical moment was broken by a police whistle at the base of the hillside. The men turned their gaze from the Parthenon to the scene playing out before them. A young man was running toward the commercial center of the city with a uniformed police officer giving chase and rapidly gaining ground.

"Someone is in a heap of trouble," said Lance.

"I think that I know that man! He looks like Remy Jovanovic," cried Nico. "He's in our international class at the Glyfada church. I hope I'm wrong, but I'm pretty sure that's him."

# 18

# Persons of Interest

**Athens; Glyfada – Friday, June 24**

Since early morning, Inspector Papadakis had been at his desk, reviewing the Bill Blevins homicide file in anticipation of his meeting with the victim's son. Many of the questions posed by Andy Blevins in his email correspondence with the inspector were the same questions Papadakis had been asking himself. *Who was suspected of being the murderer? What motive could he have had to kill Bill Blevins? Why had the corpse not been returned to the States?* They were good questions that defied easy answers.

Papadakis and his team of investigators had followed their protocols and had amassed a body of evidence, but not enough to warrant an arrest of anyone suspected of the crime. He and Inspector Baros had interviewed the four men who had dined with Blevins the night he was murdered. None had seen the American attorney after he left the Republic Dining Room. No apparent motive could be linked to any of the four. Three Americans had been allowed to leave Greece and return to the States.

The fourth was Alex Zerras, also an American who was currently a resident of Athens. None of the four men was a suspect in the case.

Two other persons of interest were Leah Melamed, an Israeli who met with Blevins shortly after he left the dinner party at the Republic, and Aleksy Jablonski, a local employee of Maritime Shipping. Both were present for the business meeting with the Americans on the morning the victim had been found slain in his hotel room. Jablonski had been interrogated at length by Inspectors Papadakis and Baros, but there was no reason to believe that he had ever met Blevins.

The coroner's report was unambiguous. Blevins had been slain with a knife, likely a dagger. He died of multiple stab wounds to the chest and a slit throat that caused him to bleed out quickly. Skull fractures were also found, the result of three blows to the head by a cylindrical metal object, a solid rod, or a pipe. Papadakis knew the answers to *who, what, how, when,* and *where.* He was still searching for answers to *why* and *by whom.*

Someone tapped lightly on the inspector's door. Andy Blevins had arrived promptly for his appointment and was being ushered into Papadakis's office by Inspector Baros.

"Inspector, this is Andy Blevins and his friend, Lance Arnold," Baros said. "Gentlemen, meet Inspector Papadakis."

The men engaged in a sobering discussion of the mysterious events that resulted in the death of Bill Blevins. Papadakis shared what information he could, being careful not to compromise the integrity of his investigation. He omitted the fact that Leah Melamed had been a "no-show" for her scheduled interview with the inspectors and that tracers had been sent to field offices throughout Greece to determine if she was still in the country.

Andy had brought a file folder prepared by his father in anticipation of the fatal trip to Athens. Memos written to the file revealed the attorney's intention to probe the issue of *price discrepancies by Jaffa Industries and excessive transport fees paid to Maritime Shipping*. The information corroborated similar reports obtained by the inspector from his interrogation of Herman Moore. He made a note to set up another visit with Aleksy Jablonski.

As the meeting ended, Andy stood, thanked the inspector for the work he was doing to solve the case, and made one final request. "Inspector Papadakis, when will you release my father's body to be sent home? My mother is anxious for that to happen soon."

"Yes, of course. I will do what I can to take care of that today."

After spending an hour with Inspector Papadakis, Lance and Andy walked out of the police station and down the street to a parking garage where Nico had been waiting in his car.

“How did it go?” Nico asked.

“Interesting discussion with the inspector,” Lance said, “but not sure he is anywhere close to solving the case.”

“He did say they will release my dad’s body to be returned to the States. That’ll please Mom.” Lance knew that Andy was anxious to share that news with Donna when he called her later in the evening.

“Any good news helps,” Nico replied. “Hey, guys, if you’re hungry, let’s find some lunch in Glyfada. I want to show you the church building and some of our community outreach programs.”

Nico took the coastal route south from downtown Athens to Glyfada, one of the capital’s largest suburbs. The views were spectacular. To the right were strands of golden beaches along the Saronic Gulf, and to the left, the foothills of Mt. Hymettus. Taking the scenic route added twenty minutes to the fifteen-kilometer trip but was well worth the extra time. The crew stopped at a waterfront restaurant where they enjoyed authentic Greek salad with fresh shellfish from the bay.

After lunch, Nico gave his American guests a tour of the church where he had ministered for twenty years. Unlike the traditional Greek Orthodox Church facilities with their prominent copulas and rounded exterior walls, this church building was strikingly plain–no steeple; no gingerbread; it was just a house of worship. Had it not been for a sign in front that read *Glyfada Beach Community Church*, the building might have been mistaken for a warehouse.

Having toured the modest facilities with his friends, Nico shared with them the church's mission and information about a few of its programs.

"I am especially pleased with the work we are doing with the international young people who live in our neighborhood," Nico began. "Many of them have not grown up with Christian parents. Nothing gives me greater satisfaction than to bring a young man or young lady to the Lord. I live and breathe for those opportunities."

"Praise God!" Lance exclaimed, feeling a special bond with Nico, a fellow worker in the kingdom of God.

"Of course, that doesn't mean that we have success with all of them," confessed Nico. "Last night, after I took you to the hotel, I received a call from the Athens police. Remy Jovanovic was the young man we saw being chased by the police officer. He was arrested for dealing drugs near Mars Hill. Before I picked you up at the hotel this morning, I stopped by the detention center and visited briefly with Remy. He feels so much shame."

"I'm sorry, Nico. What will happen to him?" asked Andy.

"From what I can tell, this is his first offense. I encouraged him to cooperate with the police. If he does, they may have him do some community service work, but not send him to prison. We have had a major drug problem in Athens for the past few years. The police are doing all they can to uncover the nerve center."

# 19

## Taurus

### Athens – Friday, June 24

A new case folder was lying on Sophia Baros's desk when she arrived at her office. A note, taped to the folder, read: *See me*. The handwriting was unmistakably that of her boss, Giorgos Papadakis.

"You wanted to see me, inspector?" she asked, standing in the door well to his office.

"Yes, come in, Sophia. Have you had a chance to look at the file?"

"Just a glance over. Another drug bust on the hill?"

"Perhaps," Papadakis said, "but it could be something much more. Last night, a police officer picked up a dealer who sold a young kid some cocaine. From the transcript in the file, the perp may be willing to *sing* if he can avoid spending time in prison. During the initial interrogation, he referred to Maritime Shipping being involved. I thought you might want to pull that thread and see where it leads. See if the chief's office will let you have a crack at him."

"Sure. I'm on it," Baros responded quickly. "I'll get back to you this afternoon."

Baros had been working with Papadakis long enough to know that if the inspector smelled smoke, there was usually a fire. She placed a call to the deputy police chief and learned that the alleged drug dealer, Remy Jovanovic, was being held, pending his arraignment or his posting bail. Her request for a brief interview with Jovanovic was granted.

Extracting oral evidence from a criminal suspect was always tricky business. Jovanovic would be wary of his interrogators. Baros knew she had no authority to offer a guaranteed plea deal, but there was nothing that prohibited her from exploring the possibility of a lesser charge with the district attorney. *That may be enough to get the information I need*, she thought as she drove to the Acropolis Police Station.

Jovanovic was a twenty-three-year-old Croat who had been living in Athens for two years. He listed his place of employment as Maritime Shipping where he worked as a stevedore on the docks. The police had no record of his having any prior arrests. He slumped in his chair as Baros began her questioning.

"Good afternoon, Mr. Jovanovic. I am Inspector Baros with the Athens Police Department. In my file, it says you may be involved in illegal drug trafficking. If that's true, are you aware of the consequences of committing such a crime?"

"Not really," Jovanovic shrugged.

"Prison, Mr. Jovanovic. Years in prison." She paused to allow the thought of being behind bars to sink into his thick skull. "You gave a statement earlier that suggested you might be willing to work with us in return for a lesser sentence. Is that true?"

"I don't know. I'm so upset right now. Can you help me?" he asked with a bit of respect.

"If I use my influence on your behalf with the district attorney, are you willing to give me more information about the ones who have been supplying you with these drugs?"

"Will that help?"

"No guarantees, but believe me, Mr. Jovanovic, if you share the information I am looking for, the district attorney will be more than happy to listen to my plea on your behalf."

Jovanovic appeared uncertain about the inspector's offer, but he knew he was not in a favorable position without someone standing up for him. Perhaps it was the advice he had received from his minister, Nico Panagos, but for whatever reason, he agreed to talk.

For an hour, Baros probed into the sordid world of drug trafficking in Athens. Although Jovanovic was only one of many dealers on the streets, he likely knew information that would be valuable in building a case for prosecuting the leaders of the illicit operation. Of particular interest to Baros was the Croat's insistence that the epicenter of illegal drug distribution was Maritime Shipping.

"Tell me again why you believe the drug ring originates at Maritime."

"Every dealer I know is supplied by the guys at Maritime. I'm surprised you didn't know that already."

"Do you know the person at Maritime who heads up the distribution?" Baros asked.

"Well, I don't know his real name, but I've seen him. We call him *Taurus*, because he's so big and mean, like a bull." An image of Aleksy Jablonski flashed through Baros's mind. She reached in her satchel and pulled out photographs of a few men who were currently under police surveillance for drug trafficking.

"Here are five photographs, Mr. Jovanovic. Do you recognize any of them as being the man you described as *Taurus*? Take your time."

It took Jovanovic no time at all to identify Aleksy Jablonski.

"Yeah! It's him. This is *Taurus*. I'm sure of it," the Croat said, pointing to one of the photographs.

It was exactly the break Baros needed. She smiled, gathered her papers, and looked directly into the eyes of her promising witness. “Thank you, Mr. Jovanovic. You have been more than helpful. I will see what I can do with the district attorney.”

The afternoon was almost over, but she needed to get back to the office before Inspector Papadakis left for the day. *Could this have anything to do with the Blevins case?* she wondered. It was a long shot, but Jablonski was now a prime suspect in the distribution of illegal drugs from Maritime Shipping, the same company Bill Blevins had suspected as being dishonest in its business affairs.

When Baros got back to the precinct station, Papadakis was in his office, packing a briefcase with files that would be his homework for the evening. Baros startled him as she burst into the room.

“Inspector, we have someone on the line, but I am going to need your help to reel him in. The dealer has identified Aleksy Jablonski as a kingpin in the local drug operation and Maritime appears to be the hub for fresh supplies of illegal drugs.”

“I thought that might be the case.” Papadakis scratched the back of his head. “You and I may need to pay a visit to Mr. Jablonski. I have a few more questions to ask him.”

# 20

# The Escape

**Athens; Crete – Thursday, June 9**

Leah Melamed's escape from Greece was a harrowing experience. Emotionally terrorized by Aleksy Jablonski's brutality in slaying the American attorney, Leah feared for her own life. She spent a sleepless night in her room at the hotel before making an appearance the next morning at the scheduled business meeting. It was all she could do to be in the same room with Aleksy, but she feared that skipping the session would have cast suspicion on her involvement in the murder. She opted to meet with Aleksy and the four Americans, feigning any knowledge of what had occurred the night before.

When the Athens police arrived at the hotel Thursday morning, the six individuals attending the meeting in the Odysseus Room were asked to appear at the police station for one-on-one interrogation sessions that would begin shortly after lunch. The investigators were trying to learn all they could about William G. Blevins and why someone would want to murder him. The sessions were scheduled with each of the six business associates at thirty-minute intervals. Leah's appointment was set for 4:00 p.m. She had failed to show.

Learning that the police wanted to visit her, Leah made plans to flee Athens immediately. She went to her hotel room, packed her duffle, and placed a call to her contact at the Jaffa Cartel. A hastily prepared plan to rescue her from Greek authorities was put in place. Her first step was to catch an Aegean Airlines flight that afternoon from Athens International Airport to Chania Airport in Crete. Hopefully, she would be in Crete before any suspicion arose concerning her failure to show up for her interview with the police.

Leah caught a ride with an Uber driver who picked her up at the side entrance of the Aristotle Hotel and rushed her to the airport. The Lebanese driver was a chatty cabby, offering far more conversation than Leah cared to have on such a distressing day. She tolerated the banter only because he was making excellent time on the way to Athens International. The trip took only thirty minutes.

With no bags to check, Leah found the Aegean service counter and purchased a one-way ticket to Chania Airport on a flight leaving at 4:20 p.m. and arriving in Crete fifty minutes later. She had been hesitant to take a direct flight to Israel for fear that her name had been flagged on an international passenger embarkation list. The next four hours she spent awaiting her flight were the longest Leah had experienced in her lifetime. She picked up a daily newspaper at the concession stand and buried her face into the newsprint.

Finally, Leah's flight was called. Trying to be as inconspicuous as possible, she tucked in with other passengers who were in line to board a small plane that was waiting for them at the end of the tarmac. Her legs were unsteady as she climbed the steep stairs that led to the plane's opened door. A lanky, male flight attendant looked at her indifferently as she stepped into the cabin. Once she found an open row and stored her duffle overhead, she took a deep breath and slumped into the cushioned seat. The first leg of her trip home had been successful, and the second leg was about to begin.

The brief flight over the Myrtoan Sea was uncomfortably bumpy, adding to Leah's angst. She was unaccustomed to flying and did not need more stress on such a frightful day. Closing her eyes, she replayed images of the gruesome slaying of the American. The thought of Aleksy pounding the attorney with a lead pipe sent shivers down her arms. *Why did it have to be handled that way?*

Upon arrival at Chania Airport, Leah rented one of only two available used cars. Both sedans were clunkers. She chose the green 2013 Fiat Punto because it had semi-automatic transmission. The rental agent gave her a crude map of the island and instructions on how to exit the airport. Once she identified Maleme on the map, Leah set out on leg three of the mission to get back home.

Following the route she had marked on her map, Leah headed west on the National Road that hugged the picturesque Chania Sea coastal communities. There was no time for sightseeing. Too much was riding on her timely rendezvous with a private jet sent for her return trip to Israel. If she wanted to see the beaches of Crete, it would have to wait for another time.

It took Leah forty minutes to drive the thirty kilometers to Maleme. Her first task was to locate the old German War Cemetery, the final resting spot of hundreds of German paratroopers who died during an invasion of Crete during World War II. According to the map, the Maleme airport grounds were nearby. What once had been a commercial airport was now relegated to a smattering of private aircraft takeoffs and landings.

Leah parked the Fiat rental near an abandoned hanger on the east end of the airfield and glanced at her watch. She had an hour to wait before the Learjet 35 was expected to arrive. *What will I do if they don't show?* It was a terrible thought and she worked hard to dismiss it from her mind.

Thirty minutes before sundown, the lights of a small jet could be seen approaching Maleme airfield. Leah made one last check of the rental car and gathered her purse and duffle. Ten minutes later she was airborne aboard the sleek Learjet and on her way home. She did not recognize either of the pilots and assumed the plane was a charter. No one offered her a drink, but she preferred it that way. A two-hour nap was the refreshment she needed most.

# 21

# Commando

**Haifa – Thursday, June 9**

After appearing before Inspectors Papadakis and Baros, Aleksy Jablonski had waited across the street from the Athens Police Station, hoping to visit Leah before her scheduled appointment. He wanted to be sure she had her story rehearsed and that it was in sync with his own. When she failed to show, Aleksy returned to the Aristotle Hotel, and ran up the stairwell to her fourth-floor hotel room, thinking she may have taken a nap and not set an alarm. No one answered the door.

Mystified by Leah's disappearance, Aleksy left the hotel and drove to his home in Piraeus. He lived in one of the many apartment units that lined the streets between the city's expansive harbor and Piraeus University. It was conveniently located near his offices at Maritime Shipping and within walking distance to local stores and service centers. Aleksy was a bachelor, living alone.

When he reached his apartment, Aleksy immediately placed an international telephone call to Ishmael Reuben, Executive Vice President at Jaffa Industries, and titular leader of the Jaffa Cartel.

"She didn't show," Aleksy began. "The bitch didn't show!"

"Take it easy, Aleksy," Reuben answered in a reassuring voice. "We've got this. She's on her way back to Israel tonight. Everything is being taken care of from this end."

"It better be! The bitch knows too much. She was there when it all came down and if she talks, we're all in trouble."

"Believe me, she won't talk." Reuben had already put plans in motion to assure all members of the Jaffa Cartel that Leah Melamed would be talking to no one–not now nor in the future.

The men spent a few minutes discussing current shipments and rebates being handled between Jaffa Industries and Maritime Shipping. With the nosy American lawyer out of the way, they were hopeful the threat of exposing their illicit drug trafficking and money laundering scheme had passed. Aleksy hung up the telephone and made himself a scotch and soda. He was emotionally spent.

# # # # # #

The Learjet 35 carrying Leah back to Israel touched down at the Haifa Airport two and a half hours after leaving Crete. Jaffa Industries preferred to use the airfield in Haifa, only one hour north of Jaffa by car, because it was easier to clear security than at the intensely fortified Ben Gurion Airport in Tel Aviv. Sde Dov, the nearest airport to Jaffa, was no longer available. It had been permanently closed in 2019, making room for a planned-unit-development, dedicated to luxury apartments and commercial retail development on the valuable land near the Mediterranean Sea.

After a smooth touchdown on the runway in Haifa, the pilot taxied the Learjet to a hangar reserved for civilian aircraft and left it with an attendant who doubled as a night security guard. The party of three then made its way to a dimly lit parking garage where Leah's two escorts took on a whole new persona. One grabbed her arm, leading her to a dark gray, Mitsubishi Outlander SUV, while the other brandished a gun and ordered her to hop in the backseat.

"What's going on here?" she shrieked.

"Shut up and get in the car!" Within seconds, the men had gagged and blindfolded Leah, tying her hands behind her back with leather cords. Her muffled protests were answered with silence.

Leah had no idea where her captors were taking her. She assumed the kidnappers were working at the behest of the Jaffa Cartel. A rendezvous with Ishmael Reuben was likely in her immediate future. All she knew for sure was the car was traveling at highway speed.

Halfway between Haifa and Jaffa, the driver stopped at a roadside convenience store to buy cigarettes and a six-pack of beer. The second man, who had been in the backseat with Leah, used the break to visit the restroom inside the store. Neither man gave much thought to leaving Leah in the car because of the restraints they had imposed upon her. She could neither see, talk nor use her hands. They failed to consider, however, that her mind was still unrestrained, and at that moment, it was working double time.

When Leah felt sure the men were inside the store, she pressed her face against the backseat window, gyrating her head and making as much noise as the gag around her mouth would allow. Her only prayer was that someone would notice her. And someone did.

As fortune would have it, an Israeli soldier who was a member of the elite Commando Special Forces, pulled his car into the space next to the parked Mitsubishi. Planning to go inside the store, the soldier saw something that stopped him in his tracks. A frantic, bobbing, masked face, was flattened against the Mitsubishi's backseat window and a muffled noise was coming from the car.

Peering through the SUV's right-rear window, the Commando saw Leah's captive condition and immediately sprang into action. All his training kicked in as he yanked open the vehicle's back door, pulling Leah's gag and blindfold from her face, and leading her from her perilous plight to safety.

The Commando turned on the ignition of his Hyundai Santa Fe, put it in gear, and sped out of the store's parking area before Leah's captors knew she was gone.

"Are you okay?" the Commando inquired.

"Not really. To be honest, I'm terrified."

"I can imagine. What was going on back there?"

Leah knew she couldn't tell the truth without incriminating herself. She struggled to fabricate a story that would sound plausible to her liberator.

"I was minding my own business at the airport in Haifa when these two men abducted me and said they were going to hold me for ransom. I have no idea who they are or why they chose to kidnap me. Thank you for doing what you did. I'll never be able to repay you."

"Where can I take you? Do you want to file a report with the police?"

"No! Not now. I just want to get as far away from those thugs as I can."

"Where's home?"

"I live in Jaffa, but I don't feel safe going there tonight." She thought for a moment about any viable alternatives. "Where are you heading?"

The Commando paused, "Well, I'm on my way to Haifa, but tell me where you want to go, and I'll take you there."

"Haifa is fine," Leah said. "I have an aunt who lives there. She will be glad to keep me until my nerves settle."

"Haifa it is," affirmed the Commando, pressing down on the accelerator.

# 22

# Weighing the Options

**Haifa – Friday, June 10**

The shock of Leah's late-night arrival at her doorstep had not worn off on Rachel Braun. As she prepared breakfast for her niece, Rachel recalled her own teenage years when she had shared a bedroom with Leah. *That seems so long ago*, she mused. The two knew each other well, although they had not seen that much of each other in recent years.

Rachel lived in a small, but well-kept home in a middle-class neighborhood of Haifa. Her husband was in the military and was currently on assignment in the Golan Heights. They had two teenage children, both currently attending a youth camp near Tiberias on the Sea of Galilee. Rachel worked part-time as a receptionist in a dentist's office. Friday was her day off.

Leah hesitated to share much of her incredible story with Rachel for fear that she would be placing her aunt in harm's way with the police, or worse with the cartel. The goons that kidnapped her at the airport were obviously hired by the cartel. They would not be satisfied until they had completed their assigned mission. And by this time, the Athens police had surely put out an all-points bulletin to find Leah in Greece or Israel. Her wick was burning low.

Responding as she could to Rachel's questions about her sudden appearance in Haifa, Leah conveyed bits and pieces about her trip to Greece and the events leading up to her decision to flee the country. Her voice trembled and her hands shook as she described her encounters with Aleksy Jablonski. Finally, she could hold back no longer and the whole narrative came gushing forth.

"I don't know what I'm going to do, Rachel," Leah sobbed. "It would be suicide for me to show up at work. These men are ruthless and as a witness to the murder, I'm a liability to the cartel."

"Why don't you share this story with the police here in Haifa?" Rachel asked.

"If I do, I'll be arrested. Then the cartel will post my bail and have custody of me. Don't you see? I'm caught in my own mousetrap."

The futile discussion and handwringing went on for more than an hour. No viable option was on the table. The more they talked, the more hopeless the situation became. Suddenly, there was a firm knock on Rachel's front door.

"Don't answer," Leah whispered immediately. She was frightened beyond words.

Rachel tiptoed to the window and peeked cautiously through the partially opened shades. "It's a military officer," she said softly. "I think it may be the man who brought you here last night."

Leah moved to Rachel's side to view the caller for herself. "Yes, that's him. I'm sure. You can let him in."

Rachel opened the door.

"Good morning, ma'am. I wanted to drop by and make sure the young lady was okay," the Commando said.

"Won't you come in?" Rachel said, opening the door wider. Leah stood at Rachel's side and slightly tucked her head.

"There you are," the Commando smiled. "How do you feel this morning?"

"I've been better, but I made it through the night, thanks to you." She raised her eyes to meet his. "And by the way, I don't even know your name."

"Martin Chambers, ma'am. And do you mind if I ask yours?"

"Leah. Leah Melamed." Suddenly, she took two steps forward and gave the Commando a big hug and a kiss on the cheek. "You saved my life!"

"I didn't do that much," he blushed. "Besides, you allowed me to use some of my training. A Commando doesn't get too many chances to be a knight in shining armor. We're usually crawling on our stomachs through some tunnel or cave."

"Would you care to join Leah and me for some coffee?" Rachel asked. "It won't take me a minute to brew us a pot."

"Yes, ma'am. A cup of coffee sounds good. Thank you."

Rachel left Leah and Commando Chambers in the living room while she prepared coffee and warmed up some pastries in the kitchen.

"Now that you've had a night to sleep on it, do you have any thoughts about who those men might have been and why they chose you to be their ransom victim?" Chambers inquired.

Leah was slow to answer his question. The Commando may have saved her life, but could he be trusted with her darkest secrets? She began to weep.

"I'm sorry. Did I say something wrong?" Chambers was bewildered by Leah's response. "May I?" He offered her a clean handkerchief.

"This is so painful. I don't know where to begin." Leah paused with her eyes fixed on the floor. "If I tell you what I know about last night, will you promise not to call the police?" A pang of uncertainty flashed through her mind, thinking that she may have already said too much.

"Yes, of course. I promise."

Leah wiped the tears from her eyes and began to unpackage the torturous tale of her involvement with the Jaffa Cartel and the murder she had witnessed two days ago in Athens. As much as she hated to admit it, the events of the past week had become a defining moment in her life. Whatever became of her from now until the day she died, she would never be able to erase the terror or the shame she felt for her involvement in William Blevins's murder. It was a permanent stain on her soul. And it hurt!

Chambers digested the story in small doses, trying not to interrupt Leah as she unburdened herself of her secret life. He showed no shock nor disgust with the sordid details. Occasionally, he nodded his head as a way of expressing his support and compassion. The pain in Leah's voice was unmistakably sincere. Every nerve in his body was aching for a woman whom he had met less than twelve hours ago.

"Leah, there may be a way out of this mess, but there is risk involved. I have a brother who practices law in Haifa. He is well connected with a few officials in the Justice Department. If he were able to get the government to grant you immunity and place you in a witness protection program, would you be willing to disclose all that you know about the Jaffa Cartel? You would need to tell them about the drug smuggling and the murder that you witnessed in Athens."

"Do you think it's possible they would grant immunity?" Leah asked with a tinge of hope in her voice.

"I don't know, but I would be glad to introduce you to Benji this afternoon and see what he has to say."

Rachel looked at Leah and nodded.

# 23

# Stakeout at the Delphi

**Piraeus – Sunday, June 26**

For the past two days, Inspectors Papadakis and Baros had been working twelve-hour shifts in Piraeus, staking out the neighborhood where Aleksy Jablonski resided. The statement from Remy Jovanovic had pointed a direct finger at Aleksy as being the principal distributor of illegal drugs to dealers who worked the streets of Athens. The officers carried with them a warrant for the suspect's arrest.

Both inspectors had knocked on Aleksy's apartment door numerous times, but no one had answered. Neighbors who claimed to have known the man said that he had not been seen for days. The officers were ready to implement "Plan-B" when a silver Toyota Peugeot 308 pulled into the underground parking garage beneath the apartment building.

"That's him," Baros cried while looking through a set of field glasses.

"Let's go," barked Papadakis.

Inspector Papadakis bolted from his unmarked cruiser and ran to the steps leading to the apartments' first floor. Baros was close behind.

"You stay here," he ordered. "Make sure he doesn't exit through this entryway or come up the garage ramp. I'll try to intercept him before he gets to his apartment."

The Delphi Apartments had been built in the early 1950s. All units in the three-story structure opened into narrow hallways that were dimly lit. Carpet, mildewed from years of neglect, left an unpleasant odor on every floor. Most tenants were retired pensioners and university students who could afford nothing finer than the Delphi and comparable apartments in the neighborhood. Aleksy was an exception. He had the money to upgrade but chose to live in the area because of its proximity to his work and because he was too tight to pay higher rent somewhere else.

There was no elevator service at the Delphi. Papadakis quickly found the stairwell and ran up the steps to the third floor. Out of breath, he ducked into a laundry room across from Aleksy's apartment and waited for the suspect to arrive.

Aleksy had left Piraeus on the same day Ishmael Ruben had reassured him that Leah Melamed was being silenced by the Jaffa Cartel. It was troubling enough that Leah had been an eyewitness to the murder at the Aristotle Hotel, but when she failed to show for her interview with the police, Aleksy was worried she might become a loose spoke in the wheel. Until he could be sure that she was unable to squeal, he wanted to put some distance between himself and the crime scene.

Maritime Shipping had offices in Patras, another Greek port city, 215 kilometers west of Athens. Aleksy traveled to those offices several times each year to conduct business on behalf of the company. Impulsively, he had decided to make an unscheduled trip to Patras, leaving the precarious situation he had been suffering through at home. After throwing two weeks' worth of clothes into a suitcase, he tossed the bag into his car and headed west on the new toll road that ran up the northern coast of the Peloponnese Peninsula. He was glad to be out of town.

The next few days were spent marking time in Patras as Aleksy allowed his nerves to calm down. By the end of the second week, he felt sure the cartel had taken care of Leah Melamed and that she was no longer a threat to expose his role in the American attorney's murder. He also felt certain that no further incriminating evidence had been found by the Athens police; after all, they had released him following his appearance at the police station, seemingly satisfied with his answers to their extensive barrage of questions. It was time for him to return home.

Papadakis heard Aleksy lumbering up the stairwell at the Delphi and opening its door to the third floor. The moment the suspect reached for his key to unlock the door to his apartment, the inspector emerged from the laundry room to confront him.

"Mr. Jablonski, I am Inspector Papadakis and I have a warrant for your arrest."

"What the . . ." Surprised by the unwelcomed appearance of the inspector, Aleksy turned and began to run back down the stairwell, taking two steps at a time. Papadakis pursued the fleeing felon but would not have caught him had Aleksy not stumbled at the landing of the first floor. The men fell into a scuffle, striking at one another, but with neither landing a serious blow.

Each man struggled for the leverage needed to put his adversary away. However, once the confrontation became a wrestling match, the advantage quickly shifted to Aleksy. The suspect weighed almost a hundred pounds more than the inspector. Pinned underneath the enormous torso of the man they called *Taurus*, Papadakis was powerless to move.

Sensing the opportunity to strike a fatal blow, Aleksy reached inside his coat for the sheath that held his lethal weapon. Papadakis, who was helplessly lying on his back, saw the gleam from the Pole's dagger, now being held high over his attacker's head. Death appeared imminent until he heard a *crack* followed by a deep, guttural moan coming from Aleksy's throat. Turning his head, the inspector saw Sophia Baros who had delivered a debilitating blow to the assailant with her nightstick.

"Sophia! Thank God it's you!"

Papadakis crawled out from under Aleksy, rolled the brute over on his stomach, and applied a pair of handcuffs.

"Inspector, I believe we may have more than drug charges to file against this man," Baros said as she wrenched the weapon loose from Aleksy's clenched fist. "Look at this dagger. Could it be the one we have been looking for in the Blevins case?"

"I think you may be on to something, Sophia. We'll send it to forensics tomorrow and see what they have to say," Papadakis said. "My hunch is that we have a match."

The officers helped Aleksy stumble to his feet. Baros pointed a taser gun at the dazed man's legs, promising to use it if he did not cooperate. With the threat of the taser and verbal prodding, she managed to get him into the backseat of the police cruiser. Her hopes were high that they had nabbed a key player in the recent surge of illicit drug trafficking in Athens, and with any luck, may have also solved the William G. Blevins murder case.

# 24

# Epilogue

Inspector Giorgos Papadakis had received a call from forensics confirming that the dagger Aleksy Jablonski had used while trying to kill the inspector was in fact the weapon that had been used to murder William G. Blevins. Microscopic specks of blood found on the knife's handle matched those of the slain American. Being able to identify the weapon was always a valuable piece of evidence for any prosecuting attorney's case, but not necessarily conclusive of someone's guilt. The inspector felt confident Jablonski would be convicted of dealing drugs; now he needed to sew up the loose ends on the capital homicide case.

Upon returning from his lunch break, Papadakis found a note on his desk with a message asking him to return a call from the Director of Israel's Witness Protection Authority (WPA) in Jerusalem. The note was marked "urgent." He closed the door to his office and placed the call.

From what the inspector could discern from his conversation with officials at the Israeli Ministry of

Public Security, Leah Melamed was seeking immunity and witness protection in return for her testimony against principals involved with the Jaffa Cartel. Specifically, she had first-hand information about the distribution of drugs, money laundering, and the murder of William G. Blevins. According to the Israelis, Leah was an eyewitness to the murder! The call to Inspector Papadakis was to see if the Greek authorities might be interested in a similar arrangement that would offer the informant full immunity from all charges in Greece.

"That's a step over my pay grade," Papadakis said, "but yes, I would certainly be willing to make that deal if I can persuade my superiors to go along. I will call them immediately." He took the names and phone numbers of the Israeli officials in the event he needed to secure more information and then he hung up the phone.

A broad grin crossed the inspector's face. It was the first time he had smiled in three weeks. He had a suspect, a motive, a murder weapon, and now, an eyewitness. His chances of securing a murder conviction against Aleksy Jablonski had just become brighter. He summoned Inspector Sophia Baros to his office.

"Sit down, Sophia. I think you will like hearing this news."

# # # # # #

A month had passed since word of Bill Blevins's murder rocked the Pecan Village community. Andy and Lance had returned home from Greece, still burdened by the tragedy of Bill's death, but hopeful that the criminal case was in good hands with the Athens police. When Inspector Papadakis called Andy to share with him news of Jablonski's arrest and the evidence that had been collected to convict him, it was an answer to the young man's prayer for justice to prevail. Although it was a poor substitute for losing his father, it allowed him and his family to move forward with their lives.

Donna Blevins was making the painful adjustment of living alone. Each of the children had spent a week or more at her house, handling calls and errands, but most of all simply being a comforting presence for their mother. Her church family had also given her good support. The Potters had worked overtime to provide Donna with cards and meals, letting her know that she had not been forgotten. She felt blessed to have so many friends who loved her and sought the best for her future.

A memorial service for Bill had been held at the church building. Lance had officiated, choosing just the right words to capture the essence of Bill's goodness as a father and a leader in the community. Every pew was filled, and a remote telecast was shown to the overflow crowd that had gathered in the fellowship hall. People were still buzzing about Mildred Simmons's acapella rendition of "Amazing Grace."

Pecan Village, as a community, was trying to process the mystery surrounding Bill's death in a place so far removed from Texas. The Rotary Club had commissioned a bronze plaque in his memory to be placed in Travis Park. Myron Williams had set up a scholarship fund in Bill's name at the high school. Each year a graduating senior would be awarded a grant to be used for next fall's college tuition. The void Bill left was enormous, but the efforts to extend his memory were many.

Lance began a series of Sunday morning sermons on how God can take the tragedies in anyone's life and turn them into something for good. *Every cloud has a silver lining* was the underlying theme of each lesson. In one sermon, he shared the Old Testament story of Joseph who was sold into slavery by his brothers, yet God used the deeds that were meant as evil to bless Joseph's kin and many others. In another lesson, Lance utilized the New Testament example of the Apostle Paul who was placed in jail in Philippi but used his imprisonment to bring God's blessings to the jailer and others in the community. The parallels were many and were not lost on the congregation that was seeking to heal.

Late one night, before retiring for bed, Lance turned to Angie and said, "Memory of the events of this past month will live for many years in the hearts of our friends in Pecan Village. Bill Blevins is a man who will not be forgotten anytime soon."

# # # # # #

As the Aspen trees were turning gold, a pair of newlyweds moved into an alpine house on Grant Lake in Crested Butte, Colorado. It was the beginning of a new chapter in their lives. They were happy. They were in love. They were ready for new adventures. Each morning the fresh mountain air smelled to them like *freedom*.

The couple had not made friends in the new community, but that could come later. For the present, they were content to enjoy their anonymity and the opportunity to get better acquainted with each other. They had met only a few months earlier under the strangest circumstances. How they came to live in Colorado was a story that would someday captivate the inquiring minds of their children and grandchildren.

"Shall we take a walk around the lake this morning?"

"Sure. I'm ready if you are."

And off they went into the woods, hand in hand, followed by their pet dog, an Australian Shepherd they had affectionately named, "Commando."

# Other Books Written by J. Terry Johnson

***Jubilee:*** a colorful pictorial history of the first fifty years of Oklahoma Christian University. (2000)

***Fairways and Green Pastures:*** A gift book with thoughts inspired by the eighteen holes of Ram Rock Golf Course at Horseshoe Bay Resort (foreword by PGA Hall of Fame honoree Byron Nelson; 2006)

***Kirby:*** A paperback memoir of a state championship baseball team (foreword by former U. S. Attorney General John Ashcroft, 2008)

***Cardinal Fever:*** A paperback memoir for St. Louis Cardinal baseball fans (foreword by MLB Hall of Fame honoree Whitey Herzog, 2009)

***Awakenings:*** A paperback coming-of-age memoir (foreword by international recording artist Pat Boone, 2010)

***Two Parts Sunshine:*** Biography and cookbook featuring Marty Johnson (foreword by former OU women's basketball coach Sherri Coale, 2010)

***10 Critical Factors in Fundraising:*** A book about raising financial support for nonprofits (Foreword by former Pepperdine University president Andrew K. Benton, 2011)

***Be of Good Cheer:*** A daily devotional book to encourage spiritual growth (2012)

***Wounded Eagle:*** A novel about Major League Baseball in San Antonio (foreword by MLB Hall of Fame honoree Nolan Ryan, 2013)

***A Glorious Church:*** A history of the New Testament Church (2015)

***Walk in Love:*** Selected quotations from the author (2020)

***My Animal Friends:*** A children's book about animals in the Texas Hill Country (2021)

***10 Essential Thoughts for Winners:*** A book on what it takes to be a winner (foreword by PGA legend Loren Roberts, 2021)

***Walk in Light***: A collection of poems by the author (2022)

- **All books available through Amazon. Search with book's title plus *Johnson.***

www.ingramcontent.com/pod-product-compliance
Lightning Source LLC
LaVergne TN
LVHW091046150826
845673LV00002B/477

* 9 7 9 8 8 3 9 7 9 5 7 6 1 *